THE
EXPERIMENT KNOWN
AS
ROSE MARIE HERNANDEZ
WILLAMSON

Louise Robertson

Brick Cave Media

brickcavebooks.com

The Experiment Known as
Rose Marie Hernandez Willamson

Cover Illustration Artist: Bryan Christopher Moss

Brick Cave Media
brickcavebooks.com
2019

For Andy and Carrie

Also by Louise Robertson

Available from Brick Cave Books

The Naming Of (Poetry)

THE
EXPERIMENT KNOWN
AS
ROSE MARIE HERNANDEZ WILLAMSON

Louise Robertson

Brick Cave Media
brickcavebooks.com

Chapter 1

Before I open my eyes, I begin the day by listening to the hum of the ship. After I open my eyes, I'm looking at the curving metal over my bunk. I think the exact color is called "gunmetal gray." I can't attest to what a gun looks like in real life—I've only seen them in vids—but I am an expert in "metal" and "gray." They have pretty much defined the boundaries of my entire existence.

Currently, my existence is in the top berth of a triple set of bunks in my family's quarters, which is the forward-most quarters, right before the flight deck of the Grimm Explorer. Fifteen years ago, it was the top-of-the-line, most high-class spaceship ever created, capable of FTL (faster than light, of course) travel.

And since then?

Since then our ship has done nothing but go. Well, for fifteen years and about nine months, I mean. We've visited Kepler-917 and Kepler-804, traveled over 900 light years, and are now circling back to Earth with one more planned stop at Kepler-526.

When I say "we've visited," I mean that some of my

shipmates have gone down and stepped on those planets. I, on the other hand, have only been near Kepler-917 and Kepler-804.

For those first two stops, there was some talk about my getting to visit a planet. It was a definite-maybe possibility. But in the end, I was too young, too small, and the equipment would not have been the right size—not even close to right, even with massive alterations. I was only four years old at Kepler-917.

I have grown a lot since then. I've been trained up (somewhat). I'm hoping that they will let me see what it's like to be on a planet and to move around somewhere with more than a quarter of Earth's gravity. Kepler-526 has about half-Earth gravity. It's a good place to try out my planet walking. I can level up on gravity again when the mission is over.

"They" are my shipmates, also known as my family and most of my friends. They are the ones who decide these things. They have all the usual variety of expertise, titles, degrees, and astronaut-like qualities. But not me. I am none of that. I am not an astronaut, scientist, or systems expert of any kind. Instead, I'm an accidental, space-faring passenger. The first and youngest accidental, space-faring passenger ever, but still just a passenger.

You already know it by now. I am passenger Rose Marie Hernandez Williamson, the girl born on a spaceship.

The mission started in 2101. It was Thanksgiving-time 2101—Friday, November 25, 2101, to be exact. You can look this up yourself.

You can also look up that I was born August 4, 2102 (by c-section, if you must know, because of the whole low gravity thing). Yes, I have done the math on when I was conceived. I think everyone on this ship and on Earth has done that math. Maybe I was conceived on Earth. Maybe. (Probably?)

You need a description of me? You do because that's not

so easy to look up due to parental restrictions on images of me. But, that description is not exciting, I promise. I am short for my age, have lots of dark, curly hair and hazel eyes—they are not green enough to be green, not brown enough to be brown. A mixed-up color, the same as my mom's.

My dad's eyes are a very dark blue. I think you have to be really paying attention to know they're blue. Mom must always be paying attention because if you ask her about them, she'll tilt her head and say, "Hmmm. Your dad's eyes are the same color as Earth from outer space."

I am sure my hair would go out in all directions just like my mom's, even if I lived in higher gravity. My mom says I should enjoy a head of hair like that. "It is a wonderful thing to have," she says. "Young people have the best hair," she says.

Is that enough of a description? Height. Eyes. Hair. Check. Check. Check. Oh, round face, like Dad's.

This space trip was not designed to be an experiment in human growth in a quarter g environment, but that's one of the things it has turned into. Now, of course, the World Space Center (or WSC), which is in charge of this mission, is studying the effectiveness of intergenerational family units as a support to the psychological health of the crew as well as the repercussions of long-term low-g and high-radiation on systemic development. All because of me.

So I'm a guinea pig, too. And, as of today, August 4, 2117, I am a fifteen-year-old accidental, space-faring passenger and guinea pig. Happy birthday to me.

Chapter 2

My first message of the day has already arrived. I have received this from Ethan Junior, my friend on Earth:

hbd

So I send this back:

hrd

He replies with a piece of punctuation:

?

I explain:

Happy regular day

Then Ethan Junior starts today's conversation for real:

dear friend unit welcome to yr 16th set of 365 earth days

Ethan Junior is Ethan O'Neil, Jr. He is also my best friend in the universe. His dad is head of information security at the World Space Center. Based on the pictures and vids, Ethan Junior and his dad look very much alike. Pale. Wide faces. Short reddish-brown hair. I would say they even have reddish-brown eyes. His dad is very tall, and Ethan Junior is getting there. But Ethan Junior is twice as skinny and looks like he's tilting a little to the right all the time.

Ethan Junior and I have a lot in common. He and his family moved from Dublin North West, Leinster (in Ireland) to Orlando, Florida, because of his dad's job. I have travelled 900 light years because of my parents' jobs. Also, he is only six weeks younger than me. All of this—plus his access to great interstellar communications tools through his dad— makes him the perfect candidate for being an outer space pen pal with me.

Yes, our parents set it up. We call it our "completely fabricated friendship" and the "longest play-date ever." And we say to each other, "We're too old for this."

I send a message back to Ethan Junior:

Thank you, friend unit. I enjoy your greetings from Earth.
The weather on the ship is particularly weather-free today.
What's going on there?

Ethan Junior:

i just got up. both parents are already out of the house for reasons relating to their jobs. another hot, muggy day. the hotness and mugginess are particularly hot and muggy today.

He knows I like hearing about the weather, even terrible weather—and there is a lot of terrible weather in Florida. His hurricane reports are spectacular adventures in driving away from his home with his family and then driving back again. And I know he likes complaining about Florida, its sea level issues, its flooding, and its hurricanes. His hurricane reports are also spectacular opportunities for him to complain about Florida. Hurricanes are usually win-win for us as long as they continue to avoid actually hurting anyone we know. Though they do cause a lot of damage and mess. A lot, I hear.

Our exchange this morning is typical. It's a good kind of typical, the kind of typical I look forward to.

Let me tell you, living your whole life on a spaceship makes everything Earth-side seem exotic and full of spontaneous sensations. To be blunt: I think I have smelled everything on this spaceship a million times. The air vent smell. The smell of recycled (and not recycled) water. The smell of hydroponically grown lettuce. Metal. Plastic. Fiberglass. I have a complete mental catalog of the textures too—where smooth is, where rough is, where you can find the flexible layers of mesh filters. And the tastes are a pretty limited inventory as well. I've eaten each of everything the ship has been stocked with or grows for this mission at east five million times.

Ethan Junior thinks it's life on a spaceship that is exotic. I think he gets to taste the amazing and unknown-to-me flavor known as "apples."

We call it even.

After getting Ethan Junior's weather report, I head to the front of the ship to see if I can hang out on the flight deck where the best windows on the ship are. This is where I take many of the pictures I send back to Ethan Junior on Earth.

Don't get me wrong. I also take a lot of pictures of the room where my parents and I have our bunks, the payload areas, and even the toilet unit—both the number 2 hole and the number 1 tube. I think I have sent Ethan Junior 1,003 pictures of the galley alone.

Today, I take a picture from the flight deck and send it. It shows a vast array of spots of light—from pinpoints to smears—white, yellow, red, and blue. An image like this can occupy my phone for at least 30 seconds. Phone to ship. Ship to Earth.

I am not allowed to post anything publicly as myself. It's not that I am a secret or that anything I do is a secret, but they are trying to make sure my life is private and not recorded like a rare eagle hatched in front of a cam back on Earth. Though, to be honest, there are a lot of cameras on this ship. We could easily record everything and post live vid round-the-clock—that is, if we had the money to pay for that kind of vid coverage. (Ah, money, kind of a myth to me on this ship, but everyone else seems to talk about it all the time.)

In fact, since Ethan Junior has a channel—just one of those free accounts on a cheap service—some of my work actually has gone public, but you wouldn't know it was me. I send him stuff with the super special WSC interstellar communications equipment, and then he sends it to a separate, non-WSC phone and uploads it from there. (If you're reading this—whoever, wherever, whenever you are—my presence on a channel can't be much of a secret anymore, and I don't think I'm leaking any confidential corporate or government information when telling you about his uploading a vid or image from a temp phone.)

Ethan Junior's username is El Gato and my username is La Gata. It's more his channel than mine, but I like being able to contribute. So we call it *Hurricanes and Rocks*. I'm the rocks part.

Chapter 3

Let me tell you more about the ship.

The spaceship's real name is WSC-1GRM-X. And, because the mission is to visit three of the nearest Goldilocks planets to Earth, we call it the Grimm Explorer. (Not too hot. Not too cold. They're just right. Get it: Goldilocks?) My dad says the people on this ship are like people everywhere. We enjoy an easy joke. Ha.

The Grimm Explorer runs mostly on nuclear fusion. We also have solar panels for auxiliary power, but they are very weak in comparison. I think the solar tech was put on the ship as an experiment and an afterthought. My dad seems to be the only one interested in it; it's like a hobby to him.

The ship's body is mostly covered with hard, glossy, white panels, with black panels below the flight deck windows at the nose of the ship and the windows next to the launch bay. Behind those panels are shutters for the flight deck and launch bay windows—in case of meteor storms. It has external fuel cells that wrap around the engine and remote control arms to help with repairs.

From the outside, when it's in orbit, the ship looks like

a cross between a killer whale and a stormtrooper. Not the kind of stormtrooper from the Star Wars films from the 2080s, but a stormtrooper from the first fifteen films. When it's in space, on the other hand, it looks like a tube. It's kind of a straight, rigid space worm—sometimes plain and sometimes with metal appendages sticking out and huge vent-like doors opening.

The magnets used to create the ship's gravity are stuffed between the inner skin of the ship and the outer skin of the ship. We have about a quarter of Earth's gravity—which is more than Earth's moon has, but still, very weak. We could crank the gravity up, but the energy cost would mean we'd lose the FTL travel and maybe the environmental system. So a quarter g is where we keep it.

We use those retractable wings for orbiting and landing— not that there's much of that going on. In fact, it hasn't happened at all on this trip. The retraction process pulls the hinged wings in and around the tube that is the ship. When extended, each of the wings is like a big stiff flipper on both starboard and port, and there's a rudder-shaped tail (also retractable) at the stern (the back of the ship), above the launch bay. (For those people who do not want to look it up, starboard is right and port is left when facing the front—or bow—of the ship.)

Looking backward along the ship from the front windows, you don't get a sense of the whole thing. You see only the white panels curving away.

Sometimes they let me put a device on one of the remote control arms and I am allowed to take pictures from that point of view. But none of those pictures show the whole thing. I have to search "1GRM-X images" to see the whole ship from the outside like anyone else. And then it's on Earth or in orbit around Earth—nothing recent, because there's no one floating out there at a good distance to take a full body shot. Note: The WSC posts that kind of stuff all the time. You can check it out yourself.

Now let's take a tour of the inside. Moving to the back of the ship from the flight deck, you go through a small anteroom, then the rooms that comprise our quarters and the other three sets of quarters. Each of the four living areas has three bunks. Each bunk has a place to lie down, straps so you don't push yourself out of bed when you're sleeping, a small locker, a little lamp, and a fan. The bunks are oriented parallel to the floor of the ship with the lockers stacked at the head of them.

I share a room with my parents, Ted Williamson and Melissa Hernandez. I have the bunk on top. Mom's in the middle. Dad's on the lowest level. Dad is prone to throwing his hands around at night, and I think that's why he has the bottom bunk—so there are fewer people who might be bothered by hands that get tossed around. Mom volunteered, I think, to be right next to him and to be right next to me. There is, ahem, another reason they want to be near each other, but I'm not going to go into that right now.

In the next room are the captain (Andre Robinson) and his wife Jack (or "Jackie") Finch. Jackie and my mom both serve as pilots and engineers and are best friends. In fact, I believed Jackie was my real aunt for the first five years of my life. I still think of her that way.

Next to that room live Panchi Ghosh and John-Michael MacFarland, also married. Panchi is a science officer and John-Michael is a payload specialist.

The fourth area is shared by Dr. Jordan Su Banks (medical person, and farm and food manager) and Sergei Stepanovich Petrov (the other science officer, cosmonaut, and part-time pilot). They are not married. They act like brothers who laugh, curse, and hang out together all the time. They make fun of each other whenever possible.

We're mostly Americans on the Grimm Explorer and it flies under the American flag. There are two exceptions to this mostly-American crew. John-Michael is originally from France (but his parents moved to the Washington D.C. area when he was three); he has a dual citizenship of some kind. And Sergei is Russian. Russia provided a lot of funding for the trip. I think we Americans had to include Sergei. But I also think we would have wanted him here even if we didn't have to have him. He's fun to be around.

Are you wondering what nationality I am? How could I be a citizen of anywhere? Technically speaking, I am considered to be an American since the ship flies under the United States flag. So if I were allowed to print out a passport, that's what it would be.

Between the living quarters and the galley is the toilet unit and shower stall (with all the sprays and suction tubes you would expect). Since everyone shares the same toilet and shower, we all take turns cleaning it—even me. I am particularly careful about wearing a mask when it's my turn for this chore. All I can think about is flying molecules when I do that. Molecules going everywhere.

When I was first included on the cleaning rotation, I would sometimes just skip my turn for the toilet and shower. I thought at the time that no one noticed. Now, I'm pretty sure someone took up the slack for me. Or everyone else was doing such a good job of cleaning that (I was right!) no one did notice. I will probably never know the answer to this question because I'm not planning to ask anyone about it.

The galley has the pantry, the oven unit, a couple of cold and hot water nozzles, and all the trays, bowls, cups, containers, sporks, knives, etc. It also has straps for holding food down in case we have to go to zero gravity. We have lots of straps all over the ship in case we have to go to zero gravity. Some things—like cups and devices—have tabs on them that stick to matching tabs on tables and walls. But zero gravity has never actually happened as far as I know.

Continuing down toward the end of the Grimm Explorer, are the areas dedicated to the experiments, 3D printing, and project work. By experiments, of course I mean all the experiments which are not me. Since we're coming around the bend to Kepler-526 and then back to Earth, the samples, and these experiments—including me—take up more room than ever.

Then, if you keep moving toward the back of the ship, you have the plant growing area, also known as "the farm." The farm always smells moist. It's vast and takes up most of the back half of the ship. The farm is full of long round metal containers which open up to reveal racks of hydroponically grown plants. The ceiling in the farm is made of tiles of grow lights that can be set to all kinds of different colors and frequencies.

We only grow carrots, potatoes, onions, garlic, lettuce, spinach, cucumbers, parsley, radishes, and dill. Does that sound like a good variety of food? Surprise, it isn't. I am sick of exactly all of those foods. Ethan Junior teases me sometimes by having a pear. Or an orange. Or peas. Or a banana. I could go on.

Also, sometimes I wish we could grow a flower, like a dandelion or a tulip.

Past the farm and all its many hydroponic containers is the medical area, sick bay, and the gym with all of our exercise equipment, weights, and weighted clothing. We sometimes wear weighted vests or arm and leg bands to help with muscle mass. Jordan would like us to wear this stuff more. I think he would sew me into a special jumpsuit filled with weights if my mom let him.

Past the places where we keep the payloads, the equipment, medication, and the storage for the ship is the launch bay. This is the only area of the ship that is closed off. It takes up the very back part of the ship and is accessed by a sealed set of doors. Basically, you come to a wall of controls and those doors. Smaller windows like the ones on the flight deck are on either side of the area right before you get to the launch bay wall so we can watch the drones, robots, and shuttle take off and come back to the ship. The launch bay itself is like a complicated version of Ethan Junior's family garage, with docking rings and extensions and no lawn equipment. It opens out into space or the atmosphere of a Kepler planet or whatever is out there.

Whatever is out there? That's the whole universe.

Chapter 4

I am expecting all three of the planets on our trip to get new names at some point, but so far they still wear the designations from the mission that found them about 100 years ago.

Ethan Junior is hoping to name them. I tell him he's delusional, and since I am the only one listening to his suggestions, there's not much hope for him. So far he has suggested everything from the Mariana Trench, the Great Barrier Reef, and the Gulf Stream to Little, Red, and Riding Hood, to combinations of the crew's names, to fork, knife, and spoon. He also wanted to name them after islands lost to rising ocean levels including Maldives, the Solomon Islands, and Micronesia. So like I said, I think he does not have much hope.

The Grimm Explorer usually zips through space at about 180 light-years per Earth year. It turns out you can't have faster-than-light travel without having the extraordinary energy capabilities of nuclear fusion technology. I read an article the other day that said they are pushing the limit for spaceships to 230 light years per Earth year. And this would be using the same technology, but only made more efficient. Still, there is nothing that could come out to meet us yet—not that we are expecting any care packages.

That's the only reason for my being the first person to be born—and really—live my whole entire childhood on a spaceship. Once the Grimm Explorer took off, there was no way to turn around, no place to stop, and no one to come pick us up. So, I am stuck here, with the low gravity, the higher radiation, and everything.

At this point in the trip, we're still a year out from swinging back around to Earth again. In a few more days we'll be in orbit around Kepler-526, the last planet we're going to visit.

The thing about Kepler-526 that makes it especially different from Kepler-917 and Kepler-804 is that it doesn't spin. Instead it faces one side toward its sun all the time while it goes around and around—this is the same behavior as the behavior of Earth's moon, which also faces one direction all the time. So Kepler-526 has a dark side and a light side and there is only a thin strip—like a vertical belt—around the planet where we can land safety. The landings (for the robots and then the manned trips to the surface) will need to be careful and precise.

Since I have studied them a lot, and since I have been close to the other two planets, and since I am on my way to the third Kepler planet where I might actually get to put my feet on the ground, I would offer the following names for the three of them: Rocks, Rocks and Mist, and Trick of Light.

Chapter 5

Do you know what it's like to do an art project on a spaceship? Think about it. Spaceships have no crayons. We have no yarn, paste, pencils, or chalk. No pinecones, construction paper, charcoal, or pipe cleaners. I've seen the vids. And I've seen all the art projects I couldn't begin to do. But most of these are fire hazards. Dust is a problem for the electronics. And it's not like we're going to have anything extra on board anyway.

Instead, we have phones, tablets, laptops, styluses, foil, putty, and plastic ties. We have water, but no paint. We have glue, but not the kind that you give a five-year-old. The scissors are in the galley and we have lots of digital (of course digital!) drawing tools. That's how I learned to write letters and numbers.

And we have space pens! Three of them! A space pen is actually a regular pen, but in space. I mean, they're also pressurized and made from tightly fitted pieces of plastic, but I'm pretty sure they're called space pens because they're used on a spaceship. If it's on this ship, that makes it a space thing. For example, I had space carrots for dinner last night—tastes just like Earth carrots. (I'm told.) But I don't get to use space pens very often.

When I was really little, I could only check the phone out from my mom or dad and use it while supervised. But everyone relaxed a long time ago and now I use devices like anyone else. The big rule is that I have to make sure that it's secure at all times. "A device that's cracked—even a little bit—is a sad, sad, sad, sad thing," intones my dad. "Never leave it on the floor. Ever. I speak from experience."

I was twice allowed to print out a special stylus for my phone and keep it (in other words, I did not have to recycle them). One is a brush and the other looks like a little rake. They are very strict about what I'm allowed to print out—and even more strict about what I can keep without recycling.

You know how I said we of course don't grow dandelions in the farm? I have spent a lot of time trying to draw them. There are plenty of stills and vid to look at. Once, I found a vid of a couple kids lying in a field of dandelions. Some of the dandelions had yellow heads, some had gray wisps. The kids were blowing the wisps all around. I think I watched that vid a hundred times just to get a sense of how it all moved around in the air and gold sunlight. Everything was burnished and gleaming like clean, stripped wires. I can't seem to get it right yet—the brush stylus helped, but I am still working on it.

Ethan Junior and I used to play games by drawing into our phones. We'd make and connect dots and lines. We'd doodle and copy cartoon characters. The games would take forever because there is sometimes a lag for images (up to a minute) and vid (up to five minutes) over hundreds of light years. The time lags have gotten a little bit better because of better software and because Ethan Junior gets upgraded stuff, but we are starting to run into trouble with my outdated equipment. When my devices and the ship finally couldn't keep up, Ethan Junior switched back to the previous device and install and he uses that as a separate piece of equipment to communicate with me.

The WSC used us to try out some of their programming so those limitations turned out to be useful information to them. Everything is always an experiment around here.

And faster-than-light communications and travel are miracles. (So Mom and Dad keep reminding me.) We just have to deal with whatever lag there is, and report anything unusual to my team leaders, a.k.a. Mom and Dad.

For Ethan Junior's tenth birthday, I sent his dad a bunch of drawings of dinosaurs and birds and he printed them out on stickers for Ethan Junior. On my eleventh birthday, Ethan Junior set up a special server on the Kraftwork multiplayer game virtual world, and decorated the Kraftwork virtual world for a birthday party. Then he and I and a couple of other kids had a four-person on-server birthday party with virtual cake, dragons, unicorns, roller coasters, and fire-breathing squirrels. There was a lot of lag on that, too. But the unicorns farted cupcakes and the squirrels were very cute. It was the best birthday party I've ever gone to. Sure, it was the only birthday party I've ever gone to, but it was the best, too.

One of other two people at the party was DeeDee Danzer, whose dad used to be one of the project managers or something for the Grimm Explorer mission. He no longer works there and I never talk to DeeDee anymore. The other kid was Maria Gene Espada, one of Ethan Junior's neighbors. I don't talk to her much, but she sometimes goes over to Ethan Junior's house and uses their WSC computers with Ethan Junior to use the vid line or chat with me.

My favorite art projects involved making dolls and animals out of foil and styluses. I wrap the plastic pieces with foil and connect them up that way, with more foil for the joints. I have to be very careful with the foil. When I'm done, I unwrap the people and dogs and cats, trying not tear anything so I can use it again and again. If I just used foil without wrapping it around a stylus, it's harder to get the figures to be really stiff and even harder to unwrap the foil without messing it up. And it's easier to make figures when you start with some kind of bones.

Before you ask, I'll answer your question: why don't I just print out figures on the 3D printer? As I said, they are very strict and this is not allowed. On the list of possible things allowed in the universe, this is at the bottom because of the "limited resources on the ship." Once, for a present, my mom printed me out a copy of a red Japanese maple leaf. And then I had to turn it back in so we could recycle it. On a scale of one to 10, we are at level 52 of "waste not, want not" and at level 78 of "reduce, reuse, recycle." We have most of the old sayings covered.

With some tape or straps to attach the foil people and animals to flat surfaces and the camera on my phone, I sometimes make short stop-motion films. I made a series about a boy who likes to make friends with lizards. I made another series about two little kids—a boy and a girl who are both named Wentzel—who get lost in the woods until of course they hear their mom calling them for dinner. They get lost a lot.

I'm currently working on a long film about a veterinarian who doesn't like animals. He is a terrible veterinarian. His customers do not like him and the animals do not fare well. The animals are rescued in the end by a different, more kindly veterinarian and the evil vet dies in the woods. I'm not sure how yet, but I'm sure there will be rats to eat him. Maybe Wentzel and Wentzel will stumble upon this grisly scene. If I try hard, I think I could make sure all of my vids exist on the same hypothetical world at the same hypothetical time.

These are the vids I send to Ethan Junior to post on his channel. We had like six views in one day a few months ago. Woo hoo. Yes, I know Ethan Junior was probably responsible for three of those views and I was probably responsible for the other three.

The foil animals were my dad's idea. Or rather, my dad's 6th grade teacher's idea. He said his teacher had them mold the foil into people and dust the figures with a little black spray paint—it made them look like sculptures. He then usually goes into a story about how popular he was in school and never fails to add that it was not easy to be so well-liked and handsome. "It can be very awkward when all the girls like you," he says.

"They have to chase someone. You were probably easy to catch," my mom always says back.

"Oh, no," my dad continues, every time. "I wasn't."

"You were for me." Mom smiles.

And Dad smiles back at her, "I was for you."

My parents are clearly into each other—I would be more embarrassed but there's no one much to be embarrassed to. All right, I get embarrassed anyway even though it's also kind of nice to know.

But about the figures I make for the vids. I have never had anything to spray onto my people and animal figures like my father had. Even if I did that sounds like something I really wouldn't have been allowed to do—fire hazard, dust hazard, chemical hazard. Hazards everywhere.

Otherwise the foil is something that works for me if I'm careful. Using anything to paint or mark it would hurt my ability to reuse the foil. So I don't think I'd use anything like that anyway and it's all for the best.

Chapter 6

I have the ultimate self-directed school experience, enforced by hundreds of light-years and a galaxy's worth of oxygen-free space.

Here's how it works.

All my school materials and assignments are delivered and created digitally. I have had a combination of school teachers and tutors who have guided me through various courses (and continue to be there for me). Also, I have been assigned a school counselor who oversees the whole thing on behalf of the Florida school system—though it's more like the counselor checks in with my mom who actually oversees the whole thing. My current counselor is Ms. Richard Elle French. Ms. French is my fifth assigned counselor and I don't really know her very well. I had a vid call with her a month ago to talk about where I am in my high school degree, what credits I still need to earn, and what I'm going to do to make up for the community project requirement I need to graduate.

Maybe I will be excused from that? I do have a good reason for it as I am hundreds of light years away from

Earth. I'm not sure if the people on the spaceship count as a community that I could do a project for. We're more like a family with many, many grownups and one kid. It's like the most extreme only child situation ever.

We use the same system that most homeschoolers use to track grades, credits, and progress—.Xtremity. (Yes, ".Xtremity" like it's an arm of the school or a subdomain or something.) It's a good network for all the subjects that I don't have anybody on board to coach me about. But it's safe to say, everyone on the ship has, at one time or another, helped with my schooling. And I end up having a lot of access to the people who work at WSC—though, to be honest, I don't have a reason to talk to them much.

This means I'm way ahead in science, math, biology, and programming. Art, not so much. But I feel like I want to do that on my own. Don't get me wrong. It's not that I want to avoid seeing what other people have done and refuse to look at art history or get any ideas from anyone else. I mean I want to explore art and try out new things on my own. That distinction might only make sense to me. But there's a sense there. I promise.

Chapter 7

Of all the things they are worried about in regards to my health, the two big ones are my immune system and my skeletal system. Spaceship life is tough on a growing kid.

These days, spaceships do a much better job at protecting astronauts from radiation exposure, so that's not as much of a concern as it used to be. But, yes, I get checked several times a year. So does everyone else on board the ship. I'm not special on that point.

But I have broken bones three times.

Is that dramatic enough? If you like, I can make it sound worse even though I feel like I've had the most boring life ever.

The broken bones are partly because of not having enough gravity. And while breaking my bones three times might seem like a lot, it is actually a pretty good number considering how freaked out everyone is about my bone density.

Maybe I'll end up having a crumpled, weak skeleton because of it. My body will be like a crushed paper bag, with gnarled fingers, spine, and legs. So I take bisphosphonates to help try to prevent that and exercise about two and a half hours a day, according to the doctor's orders. That's also according to my mother and father's orders. And, to be fair, everyone on board also exercises obsessively. Maybe we are all worried about becoming crumpled humans.

I hate lifting weights the most. So boring. Sometimes I wear the weighted clothes instead—it's easier to forget that it's good for me that way.

My mom used to turn exercising into a counting game and sang songs to me to learn numbers in English and in Spanish. I might not sing them out loud anymore, but I sing them in my head when I'm lifting. One two uno dos. One two uno dos. One two uno dos. No, I don't speak Spanish, not really. With Sergei around, I know about as much Russian as I do Spanish. One two, ahdeen dva, one two, ahdeen dvah.

When I was really little, Mom would get me to exercise with a game she made up where she would sing about moving around in the world. And I would then try to move around in that way. Like she would sing, "We slither in the morning; we slither in the night!" Then I would squirm around in my best attempt at slithering. Or she would sing, "Cats meow! We all meow!" And I would raise up my chin and meow as loudly as I could. In this way, we would burrow and preen and bark and hop through an afternoon. I really liked trying to hop like a kangaroo in low gravity. I'd curl up my body and stretch it out way too far—it feels a little out of control when I do this, and that is a good feeling in a place where everything is measured and timed and part of an experiment.

Exercise now looks like running on a treadmill or riding on a stationary bike or pulling weights on a weight-lifting machine. Before you start to think I am just like a giant gerbil in a giant gerbil habitat, I also bounce around off bulkheads like a rubber ball sometimes. My mom says she hates this, but tolerates it because, "After all, it is exercise."

Okay, sometimes I still feel like a giant gerbil in a giant gerbil habitat.

The bouncing off bulkheads was how I fractured my left arm when I was five years old and one of the reasons my mom hates it. I hit the wall and twisted my ankle after which I careened into the ceiling, slamming against it so hard and at such a weird angle, that my forearm fractured. So. Much. Pain. The ankle and the arm.

Before that injury, I fractured my left leg when I was eighteen months old. At the time, I was just starting to sleep in a bunk by myself. Mom and Dad say I was trying to get out of the bunk while they were sleeping. I caught my left leg in one of the straps and pulled and twisted at the same time. I don't remember it, but I'm assuming it was very painful also. They tell me that even in space, babies heal fast.

And last week, I broke my toe. So of course, that one is still burning clearly in my memory. It was early in the day. I woke before my mom and dad, undid the sleeping straps and popped out of my bunk thinking, "I have so much to do!" Then—smack—the side of my foot hit the corner of the bunks and everything seemed to blitz out with light and pain.

Have you ever seen a toe at a ninety-degree angle from its foot? That was what my toe looked like. When it happened, I yelped and that woke up my parents (and everyone else). I started that day with so much to do and it quickly turned into a day of doing very little and waiting for people to help me.

Jordan (Dr. Banks), as the official MD on board, did the honors of yanking my toe back into alignment while my parents held me in place. You'd think they'd use some kind of painkiller for this, but no—"It's not worth it," said Jordan. Easy for him to say.

I think yanking it back in place was worse than breaking the toe in the first place. I'm not sure, and I am not signing up to do it again to make that assessment.

If you've been keeping track, that's one fracture or broken bone every five years or so. If I live to eighty years old, I have seventeen more breaks to go.

Chapter 8

I think you probably have figured out that I count things a lot. I make mental inventories. If I'm thinking about something, I'll see if I can make a catalog of its qualities. If I have to wait for something, I'll probably be making a list in my head to occupy myself—of colors or sounds or shapes or whatever. (You know more people than I do. Does counting make me different from most people?)

And that brings up the smallest list I have. My list of people.

Most of you have whole cities of people at your disposal. How many is that? A city is like a million people? I have a spaceship of people, which is nine including me. Add to that Abuela, Ethan Junior, Ethan Senior, and Maria Gene. Also add into that group, I guess, Ethan O'Neil Senior, Ms. French, and DeeDee Danzer (who I haven't talked to in four years). That's fifteen people who I know personally who aren't me.

I can't just open the hatch, glide outside, and find someone new. I can't go to a park or coffee shop or even school for that matter and bump into a friend or acquaintance. Can you do that? I think it would be hard to get out and talk to strangers. Is that hard? Or maybe the hard part is driving, walking, or running to parks, shops, and school.

I have people around me. But I have no people around who are my age. I'm loved. But I'm not loved like a girlfriend, if you know what I mean. I'm cared for, but not understood. And I'm the first and only person like me, stuck for their whole childhood in a small place, light years away from every other human place.

That's it. That's what I have, people-wise. Counting them doesn't make them more. It doesn't make them less either.

Chapter 9

I'm going to stop and talk about this only once. Pay attention because I'm not going to dwell on it. Deep breath. Here goes. This bit here is about getting my period. I'm sure everyone reading this is going to wonder about it and some might be afraid to ask. But after I talk about it, that's it. Okay.

First of all, I didn't get my period until I was 14 years and two months old, which Mom says is a little late, but nothing to worry about. And then it happened just like it happens on Earth, I'm sure. I was expecting my period and not expecting it at the same time. There it was. A red spot on my underwear. Since that time, I've been handling it with cloths—very old-fashioned, I've read about it, women did this for hundreds of years. I take a plastic bag, put some water and soap in there with the cloths, and that is my tiny washing machine. Then they go into the regular clothes sterilizer. And done.

I know that Panchi and Jackie use some kind of medical injections to get around having a period. My mom started doing that a year or two after I was born. They don't have enough for me, though. Besides, the other women on this ship are in relationships. I'm barely a grown up. So I don't get the injections and I'm the only one around here who has to deal with getting a period. Lucky me.

Chapter 10

When the Grimm Explorer reached Kepler-917, I was only four years old. I vaguely remember feeling excited and confused. But I also have two distinct memories.

One of those memories was me watching Mom and Jackie pilot the robots remotely. I couldn't see much from the back of the flight deck (which was very dark to me at the time) where I was supposed to stand quietly—or else I would have to go to my bunk. I was holding a little rabbit toy that my mom had made out of a sock. (It was basically a stuffed sock with floppy ears sewed on.) Everyone seemed tense and the room seemed muffled. (That's what I thought, "muffled.")

Memory two is a nicer memory. Dad held me up to the windows next to the launch bay and we watched Mom and Jackie fly out of the ship. I waved at the shuttle. If I remember right, Dad kept saying, "Look—there's Little Bear! Mom and Aunt Jackie are taking Little Bear all the way down to the surface."

And believe me, the surface of Kepler-917 was a shockingly vast expanse of land to little four-year-old me.

We were very close to it. Seemingly dangerously close. I was sure we were going to bump into it. I had to keep myself from telling Sergei and the captain to watch out for the planet.

By the time we arrived at Kepler-804, I was eleven years old and a seasoned veteran not only of space travel, but also of visiting planets. It still kind of freaked me out about how awfully close we were to it and how big the thing was.

You might think it's like a festival when we get to a planet, but, no, it's all work for the crew. For Kepler-804, I got in the way a lot, so I sulked and went off by myself during the part where we sent down drones. I hid in the farm under some of the growing containers. There I made a vid of a mama dog explaining to her puppy why she shouldn't go into the pond by herself (because of drowning, of course). It wasn't a stop-motion vid. It was a series of still images that I turned into a vid with a tool on my phone. Voiceover courtesy of me. Yes, the puppy falls in the lake at the end. Yes, everyone gets wet. Yes, no one is hurt. End scene. Very basic.

I was able to get over my sulking in time to join the rest of the team to watch Mom, Jackie, and Sergei fly down to Kepler-804. I won't lie. It is a very cool thing to watch the shuttle leave from the ship and fly free, curving down to the planet surface. I'm glad I didn't miss it that time.

Chapter 11

We don't always eat together. But since tonight is a birthday night, the entire crew will come together for a special meal. That's nine people crammed into the galley at the same time. And it will be fantastic.

Birthday meals are all laid out according to the meal charts. We start the meal together and talk and eat and finish together. All nine of the birthdays are celebrated like this. They have become our own ship-wide holidays. Sure, we have some other special events that coincide with Earth holidays, but I like the birthdays best because they belong just to us.

Okay, yes, also, my birthday is treated as extra-special since I am the only kid around. And sure, yes, I like the attention. This year, I requested ramen, and Jordan (who oversees the food plans) and my mom and dad agreed to it. The noodles are vacuum-packed with the broth and there is a limited supply. It's my favorite.

We gather at 1800 hours. (This corresponds to Florida-time because it's easier to be on the same schedule with them, and it hardly matters in space where Earth's sun is in relation to where we are). My mom and dad set everything up. They picked out a three-course meal (the lettuce and carrot salad, ramen, and fruit gel for dessert). Then they split everything up according to our ration plan and decorated the table with ribbons made from torn clothes. I swear this all looks very nice, makeshift ribbons and all.

Mom and Dad are in the galley when I arrive and sit in the place of honor.

Mom says, "The birthday girl is here! I've got a vid call set up with Abuela later. She wants to congratulate you! I think she is still trying to make up for you not being able to have a quinceañera."

"Okay," I answer her. "Should I take a picture and edit it so I have a pink dress on? Got an image of a dress I can use?"

"No, no," Mom says, "That's fine. She will get over it."

The captain and Jackie come in next and fit themselves in next to my parents. "Ted, Mel," the captain says and nods to each of my parents.

Jackie is laughing already, "This looks great!"

Sergei arrives, singing in Russian. You can hear him all the way down the ship's corridor. Then Panchi and John-Michael join us. And last comes Jordan, with his big shoulders and round head, looking like he just finished a workout, all shiny and smiling.

The captain starts with a little speech. Of course he's going to say something, he's like that, but he usually keeps things to the point. He stands, straightening out his almost-two-meter-tall frame and begins, raising his drink container. "Here's to Rosie. Our voyage has been made much more interesting because you are with us. Cheers!"

More interesting. Huh. That's actually praise from the captain. He's not known for his emotionality.

My mom puts her arm around me, my shoulder tight against her. Her warmth is like a seam that sews us up as two people together. I feel like she wants something different for me than a life on a spaceship. I also sometimes feel like I want to push away everything she wants for me, including her ideas about who I am. It's like she knows me really well, but still gets it kind of wrong. But, there it is: her warmth is a seam that sews us up as two people together.

And now, instead of presents—of course, there are no presents—everyone tells a story. As usual, at my birthday dinner, people tell me about their birthdays when they were kids. My mom says her mother once made a cake in the shape of a castle with gray icing because that's the color of castle walls. The cake was very rectangular, she says. Dad tells me about being a twelve-year-old magician at his little sister's birthday party. He set up a stage in the basement and everything.

Then Dad gets teary and announces that he didn't really ever know anything about liking and loving someone till he met my mom. And then me. "So much love for you two," he says. This happens every year and on both of our birthdays.

Sergei takes this time to lecture us about celebrating name-days which are on the feast day for the saint for whom you were named. I ask, "Do I get two name-days because I was named for my mom's sister Maria and my dad's sister Rose?"

He replies, "Are they saints?"

My dad interjects, "If you ask them, they are!"

The meal itself doesn't last that long. But the stories do. And the laughter.

There really isn't a lot of extra food on this spaceship. At lift-off, they provisioned the ship with food and allocated a growing area to produce supplemental food all with the idea that there were going to be only eight people on the ship.

But since my mother first realized she was pregnant, the plans had to be flushed out the chute into the dark outside. While pregnant and nursing, she had to eat more calories a day, and everyone else had to eat fewer. And then they had to make room for me. Jordan and the WSC team re-did a livable plan for eating. They revisit the meal plans monthly, too. I know it's been a sacrifice and it's meant lost weight and hungry times for everyone on board ship. Rosie-the-diet, what a pain.

This might be the first time in history that being hungry is a tribute to new life. That's what all the adults around here tell me. I try not to complain and I try to be grateful. But I forget most of the time. And to be honest, it is tough to remember to feel like a charity case all the time. I just feel like me, no charity required.

Chapter 12

Clothes. Sigh. Of course, my clothes are made from everyone else's clothes. They've been taken in and re-done, and let out and re-done again. They are very recycled. Space fashion turns out to be borrowed, jury-rigged, and shared.

My mom and dad have taken over a lot of the clothes making and repairing. They turned it into a regular thing. On Wednesday nights at 2000 hours in the project area, they talk, plan, and sew together. They usually snicker and call it "date night." Sometimes the captain and Jackie join them for a "double date night." It turns into a kind of partner swap night, though, because my observation is that Jackie and my mom kind of pair off to talk and the captain and my dad kind of pair off. They seem to like it that way.

So my clothes have come from re-fitted clothes donated by others and altered during date nights. Last year, my mom was focused on making my spacesuit. She really wants me to be able to go down to Kepler-526. It's kind of obvious, but she's trying to play it cool because there are a lot of things that could prevent that, including basic caution.

It's exciting to think about, and scary at the same time, even when I'm guessing it won't happen.

Even though I have trained on procedures and knowledge for planet walking, realistically, I wouldn't be able to do it without a well-fitted spacesuit. Besides me, the smallest person on this ship is Panchi. But the person least likely to use their suit is Jordan. So while it would be easier to re-fit Panchi's suit, she might actually need it for herself. So they've opted to use Jordan's but with Panchi's boots. She can still use them, too, if necessary. We're sharing them.

Except for the spacesuit, I am generally not interested in clothes or making clothes. I re-hemmed my pants once to prove that I could do it and that was it. The characters for my vids are rarely made of cloth. And even when I was little, I spent many of my Wednesday nights taking pictures of needles and thread—very close up pictures of needles and thread. I tried to make some of the pictures look like the stars in space with pins and bits of clothes for the celestial objects. Some Wednesdays I hung out with Jordan on the farm or with Sergei on the flight deck. These days I make sure to stay away from date night and read, or message back and forth with Ethan Junior.

This gives my parents time to be alone without me. I know the date nights are really and earnestly a way for my parents to be a couple that can talk and live as a functioning pair. I think I was eight or nine years old before I realized they might want to hug without me around, also.

Yes, I thought of it as just hugging when I was nine years old. Yes, now I know there's probably much more than hugging going on.

My parents really dig each other and that includes one-to-one connections. You know, girlfriend-boyfriend stuff. Oh, I'll just say it. I think they are getting with each other every date night. Oh, geez. I can't even say it. You know what I mean though, right—parents getting together.

Together. Like in the vids.

It is easier to see the other couples on board being romantic with each other. Is that because I'm an outsider? With Mom and Dad, I make a family. With Andre and Jackie, I am a mood killer and I usually know when to leave the room.

But rest assured, when I realized that, I also realized when I should pretend to be a very heavy sleeper.

Chapter 13

Hello, Ethan Junior! Want to see something black and blue and brown all over? Here's my toe.

It is the day after my birthday dinner and I am sending Ethan Junior an image of my now dark brown and purple foot. The bruise looks like it's made of nebulas spreading under the skin.

wth rosie that is very gross and you need to cut your toenails

I reply:

I'm glad I can show off to someone. Everyone here is not impressed.

His message back to me:

how did i become the captive audience? everyone there is stuck with you

Mom comes into our quarters and starts putting away the bedding she's carrying. "How's that toe?" she asks.

"I'm sending pictures of it to Ethan Junior," I tell her.

And she says, "Rose Marie, that is very gross."

"That's what Ethan Junior said!" I protest.

"I knew he was a good kid," she replies.

I start to wrap up the toe again, winding the strip of fabric around the toe next to it, turning that into a convenient splint.

"Is it still getting more purple?" she asks. "You should go show Jordan to make sure that's okay."

I tell her I will and message back to Ethan Junior:

Mom is here and agrees with you about my very gross toe. Also I have to work on some trig lessons. I'll message you later.

"Mom, can I have some pancakes?"

"Yes, and after that, you need to work on the math unit."

"I just told Ethan Junior that. Don't worry, I will. I'll do it after breakfast."

When I go over to the galley to microwave some pancakes, Panchi is there sitting at the table reading her phone next to her spork and her empty tray.

Panchi looks up, says, "Good morning," and looks back down again.

"What's going on?" I ask.

"No matter how this election in India turns out, they are going to have a silly person as prime minister. It doesn't matter which party gets the most votes. I am surprised there is no one better available to lead any of the parties," she says. "The parliament is going to be messy."

I go over and get out two pancakes and put them in the microwave for 45 seconds. They come out half warm. I try for another 45 seconds.

"I think the microwave isn't working again," I say.

John-Michael comes in, leans over, and kisses Panchi on the cheek. He turns his face to her face and says, "Hi, honey. What's going on? How's Earth doing?"

"The usual, my love," she replies, swiping her hand across her phone. "Oh, the Mars colony is doing better. People seem to care about it this year. Maybe not so much next year. There's talk of another probe to Venus."

"Venus and Mars. Mars and Venus," John-Michael

answers her in a sing-song voice. Hands still on Panchi's shoulders, he swivels his head to me and says, "Hi, kiddo."

Sergei teases me and says I should hate being called "kiddo." But I, to be completely honest and serious, do not feel one way or another about it. I believe it is not really meant to make me feel little or belittled. Instead, I think that it is an awkward term acknowledging me as a young person whom John-Michael likes, but is not related to, and (on top of that) is not sure how to deal with. Something like that.

And somehow, Sergei's teasing is like this too, a way to show he likes me as a young person in a benign way. It seems like he's better at dealing with people than John-Michael—or Panchi for that matter, who is usually paying attention to work or trying to pay attention to work.

John-Michael straightens up and talks to Panchi again. "We're going to have to do repairs on gyro number 2. It isn't turning anymore. I hope it's just a matter of cleaning it out."

"The microwave might have that power problem again," Panchi answers John-Michael without looking up. "When it rains, it pours."

Here's a good example of my weather: It's metaphoric, not atmospheric. I have to say, of course I've heard rain. I play the sound of it for white noise a lot. I can practically feel it spark and tick against my arm and neck as it plinks on the metal roof where the sound was recorded (or where the sound was composed with a machine). I have of course seen rain in vids. In this one movie, a boy scooped it out of a wooden barrel with a tin cup and drank it. I can imagine the taste of water in a tin cup. But I can't imagine the taste of the water from a wooden barrel. And for sure I don't know what it smells like.

My mom says rain smells, "Fresh." "Fresh" water is not a scent I know. Recycled, I know. Canned. Frozen. Heated in a mug. Squirted into my mouth or slurped up. These tastes I know. But fresh? I can't imagine it. Also, I would love to know what people mean when they talk about the taste of water they drink from a backyard hose. It sounds dirty and as if there might be a tiny spider or two involved.

John-Michael tells his wife that he'll look at it tomorrow. "Is it just the power level?"

Panchi—still looking down—says, "I think. Rosie, did you notice anything else? Tell John-Michael what you noticed."

"Nope," I say. "It just took 45 extra seconds to cook my pancakes. Double the usual amount of time."

I take the aforementioned pancakes, one in each hand and eat them that way, not wanting to bother with sporks or trays. Syrup is too much of a mess. I like them plain anyway.

John-Michael starts to move toward the back of the ship, where I suppose he's going to prepare for gyro repair. But Panchi stops him with a question.

"Message me when you're done? Yes? Please?" she asks.

"Can't. My phone's on a direct oobi port sync in my bunk. That'll be another few minutes. Would you bring it back to me when it's done? Yes? Please?" John-Michael answers her.

Panchi turns her face up. "Sure. But it'll cost you," Panchi says and smiles at him and raises an eyebrow.

"For you, anything. I'd do anything for you, dear," John-Michael smiles back at her. "How about a kiss as a down payment?"

Without waiting for her answer, John-Michael kisses her cheek and continues his path to the back of the ship.

Panchi returns to her phone, swiping through the news feed, but now with a little grin on her face. And my ears are hot.

I know that was supposed to go over my head. I think they think I'm still a seven-year-old child. But I can see something here, a connection with someone that buzzes in the air with heat like a small motor. Panchi does not look at people's faces much. Not even John-Michael's. But I don't think she needs to. She and John-Michael are so wired to each other.

Do not get me wrong here. I am not crushing on either of them. They—and everyone else on this ship—is over forty. Forty. I am the alien life form known as young person.

But I'm young, not stupid. To describe the feeling I have watching them, I would have to say it's sweetness mixed with sadness mixed with frustration mixed with hope mixed with feeling left out mixed with dreaming of the future. I want that for myself.

What do I do now? Go study trig? Message Ethan Junior? Goof off?

I stuff the last of my pancakes in my mouth and wipe the tips of my fingers on my pants. I think math is not the next thing. Maybe download a book. Maybe go to the farm and daydream.

Chapter 14

When I pass through Jordan and Sergei's quarters on the way to get my phone so I can have something to read (or pretend to read while I think about things), I call out to Jordan—who is reading (or daydreaming) on his phone—that I am supposed to have him look at my foot later. He grunts and says I should check back this afternoon. Sergei is elsewhere in the ship, probably on the flight deck.

But, when I go through Panchi and John-Michael's room, I smell something weird.

Something off. Something new.

You know how many sensations there are on this ship? Someday I will count them. Which is to say, they are countable. Which is to say, there is a limited number of sensations on this ship.

I am sure I have a mental catalog of all of them. I could make a list of all the smells, tastes, and textures in my known world (my known world equals the Grimm Explorer plus the vid and images it receives from Earth). So a weird smell or an off smell to me is more than weird or off, it is extraordinary. This smell, right now, in Panchi and John-

Michael's room, is sharp and metallic and like fuzz in my nose.

I keep going, back through the captain and Jackie's room (no one there), back to our room. My mom is still there, writing on a tablet or sorting through reports. I'm not sure what she's working on.

"Hello, I'm back here to get my phone," I announce. I get into my bunk with it, log in to the school lesson tracking system to see if there are any good books or short stories among my assignments and to get the trig problem just in case I want to get back to that. I start to scroll through the lists for my courses and special study units.

"Oh, good," my mom mumbles.

I am done with all of my current literature assignments, but still have the trig lesson and five problems for the homework part of that. Ethan Junior was talking about some new serial he's reading—maybe I should pull that. I roll through a news feed, though I am not interested in it. Then it occurs to me to say something about the smell in the other quarters.

"It's weird," I say.

My mom says, "Something is weird about your trig assignment?"

"I'm not sure. I mean, no. I mean, it's not about the trig or anything. There was a funny smell in Panchi and John-Michael's room."

"Funny?"

"It smelled kind of tangy in there," I say.

My mom starts from her seat. She moves really fast through the room. She hits open her locker and pulls out her fireproof blanket. Then she thumbs the com on her phone, taps the all-crew icon and then, she's yelling. "Possible fire in number three quarters. Possible fire in number three. Repeat. Possible fire in number three quarters."

I shrink into my bunk. I do not know what to do. My mother's face is as stiff as when I broke my arm, all of her features are tight and pulled back into a mask of fear and focus on the possible crisis.

The captain comes pushing through from the flight deck into our quarters, followed quickly by Jackie.

I hear my dad's voice come through on all devices, "I'm in the back experiment room. I'll pull retardant from payload four. On my way! On my way with fire retardant."

I am still stuck somehow. Now the alarms are blaring everywhere. My phone—all the phones and tablets—are lighting up. Finally, I snap out of it and jump out from my bunk while pulling my fireproof blanket from my locker.

The captain and Jackie were the only ones up front on the flight deck. I hear the group converging in Panchi and John-Michael's quarters.

I stop at the doorway watching the scariest thing I have ever seen: smoke.

A grayish, transparent cloud fills the room. The three bunks are blackened. The lowest (John-Michael's) is completely charred and melted-looking. The floor next to it has brown and black spreading out in front of it. The lockers have doubled over like they have been punched in the stomach. Panchi's bunk—the middle one—is almost as bad as John-Michael's. The top bunk is charred and buckled in the middle, hanging down (like someone's butt in a hammock) into the next bunk.

My dad is spreading white flame retardant powder over the still-smoldering bunks, on the bedding that's now on the floor, and near the walls of the quarters.

It reeks of metal and plastic. It's a sharp, oozing, putrid smell.

My mom, the captain, and Jackie are on this side of my dad, closer to me. With their fireproof blankets, they're on the floor looking for hot spots. Panchi and John-Michael are doing the same on the other side of my dad. Sergei and Jordan's faces hover in the doorway opposite me.

My dad holds up a phone and it is completely warped.

The glass is cracked. The thin casing around the edges is crumpled. The back of the phone has split from the rest of it and you can see the slivers of computer chips and cards. The direct oobi sync cord hangs off like a tail and the soft plastic around the wires is peeled back.

Everyone looks up, and then John-Michael alone looks down, his head and neck lowered almost to the ground where he kneels.

Jackie's hand flies to her mouth. Panchi's hand and arm move around John-Michael's back.

Dad says, "This is it. Have we got it all? Everyone?"

"Everybody," the captain commands. "We need to check all the cords and devices. Ted, you stay here and triple-check the quarters for hazards and anything still hot. I want all your observations on the scene of the fire as soon as you can get them to me. Then check the system networks for any problems."

True to form, the captain is in order giving mode. All crewmembers are all going to get assignments. Yeah, I'm not going to be in that. I'm a bystander and experiment, remember?

Dad nods and the captain continues.

"John-Michael, get everything touched or affected by the fire and take it to experiment room two to be inspected. We're going to treat it all like evidence. Make an inventory of all of that. Jack, you and Mel run diagnostics on the ship. We need to check the ship, hull integrity, wiring health—everything. Jordan, go with them to make sure we're checking all areas of the ship for air chemistry. We're going to need to verify that the experiments are still sound—Sergei and Panchi, you all start that process."

He looks around the room. "Everyone, after this is cleaned up, get any hand-held devices that have been issued to you, as well as any oobis, other syncs, lines, or cords, and take them to the back experiment room. Tablets, phones, cameras, adapters. We need to go over all of it for problems. All of it."

Then he does something astonishing. He turns and looks at me. "Rosie. I'm going to want you to start a list of all this equipment. The devices, oobis, and other sync equipment. All of it. We want a good inventory of what has been checked, what's damaged, and what still needs to be reviewed. We have a list from when the mission was deployed. You can start with that. Download it off the ship's network; it's stored with the system manuals."

It is my first order. I mean, first official order. Am I crew? Am I staff? Am I still a glorified passenger? I've been told to do stuff before. I take my turns at cleaning and other chores like everyone else.

But this is not a chore or exercise or schoolwork. It's from the captain. And what is my first response to my first order? Surprise and fear and immobility and disbelief. I'd never had to do anything like this on my own before. Usually, I am an assistant—and an extraneous one at that. I've been given a lot of make-work so far in my life.

Then I realize this order is do-able. I know where to look for the mission inventory and I could make a list from that. I could use a spreadsheet to track each item, and whether or not it had been checked in. If it was damaged, I could make notes on how damaged. I think a picture of each item would be good, too, as a reference to its status after the fire. And so I look straight at the captain and nod.

Looking around these quarters at the charred stuff, the singed bunks, and the floor, I feel better.

But the air still smells terrible.

Chapter 15

I haven't spent a lot of time in the back of the ship by myself, but here I am doing something that feels like it matters a little. And a little bit of mattering is more than I usually feel—which is like I'm an extra person if you've forgotten already.

After my dad shows me the device inventory documentation on the ship's network, I set up a separate list of handheld devices. Now I'm working on marking which ones are still accounted for and unaccounted for. First, I mark the phone that started the fire as "Destroyed." Then I go to the serial number for my phone and mark it as "In Use." Now John-Michael will get another one of the spares to use as a personal device. In this way, one by one, I plan to check on everything on this list.

It is especially quiet back here because we've dropped out of FTL speed. There's no hum in the Grimm Explorer. That really adds to the empty feeling. It almost feels cold.

So, before settling down to work, I get into the WSC system. Most of the time, I'm messaging people on a com or responding on some fake-name social media account, but with the WSC we all still have an account to write to each other and send information.

Other than WSC people, I think I have only exchanged formal messages with Ethan Junior and my school counselor. And with Ethan Junior, it was years ago. Literally. I think it has been years since I sent anything to him that way—and I think that was a joke to test the account.

Also in my WSC account is junk. Yes, I get anonymous messages and ads like anyone else. You'd think I'd be more able to stay under the radar since I'm only allowed to use this to send messages to other WSC addresses, but I'm not. Usually the filters sort out most of them before I see them, but today I have two suspicious messages.

The subject line of one of them asks if I'm worried about my aging metabolism. I just hope I can get to the point where I have an aging metabolism. Delete.

The other message looks like it's from a news feed— weird because I do not sign up for that stuff. Its subject is "Today's Headlines." I do not remember signing up for this, but you know the news, it live-pulls its headlines from other places, with its constant stream of trends, repurposed posts, and celebrity names. Blah. Blah. Blah. No original content found.

I tap it open by accident and it partly loads. Then: nothing. No message—just a gray background, but my phone starts to spin. The little circling icon shows that it's processing something.

Now I have that same feeling I had when I smelled what-turned-out-to-be John-Michael's burning bunk. In other words, this doesn't feel right. I hold down the reset button to do a hard shutdown of the device.

I think I did something really, really not good.

Jordan enters the room. Immediately, he says, "What's wrong?"

"I don't know," I say. "But I accidentally opened a

message from some news feed and my phone started spinning."

"Crap. I'm going to get your dad in here." Jordan thumbs the com on his phone. "Ted, can you get to the experiment room. We have a potential network breach." Jordan looks at me and smiles. "Don't look so sheepish. This happens to a lot of people. You did the right thing by shutting that thing down right away."

Dad comes sliding into the room, looking at both of us. "So what's going on?"

Jordan tells him about the possible virus. I say nothing, face hot, chest heavy.

"Okay," Dad tells us. "Let me check the security on the network and then we'll get to your device."

He logs into the system and starts running diagnostics. Jordan and I watch him. Jordan asks me for more information about what happened.

"It said it was from a news feed? Did it say which one?" Jordan asks.

"I don't know," I say. "The subject said something about today's headlines. I was just trying to delete it without reading the thing and hit it open by mistake."

But what I'm really thinking is how fast I went from feeling useful and not like a waste of space (for once) to feeling like the exact opposite.

My dad says, "I think it was a known virus and there won't be any problems with the ship's system. We'll keep running the diagnostics, but I want to take a look at your phone. You shut it down right away?

"Yeah," I reply. "I didn't know what else to do."

"Okay, let me see it." He powers it on again.

The room is silent. And the room and the silence seem to be growing. I have the feeling of static in my head and that is loud and getting louder.

"We're going to have to wipe this. I'm sorry, honey. I think it's an old virus that corrupts all your tools and data. Actually, after we wipe this, we'll check it again. In the meantime, you'll get a new device. Do you also need a lecture about not opening anything from anyone that's not from a WSC address?"

"I know I shouldn't have, but it was an accident."

"That's two devices in two days. Wow. We are going to run out if this keeps up. Of course, I can refurbish yours and maybe print out new parts. We probably have specs for a whole new piece of equipment. That would be fun to make. Okay, so you know we won't actually run out. I'm setting up a spare phone for John-Michael's personal device now and after that, I'll get to something for you. Uh, it might be a day or two with everything else. Talk to the captain about that inventory you were working on. See how much you can do without a handheld device."

Now that is not a conversation I want to have.

Captain Andre Robinson might be married to my mom's best friend, and we live on the same ship, but he always seems remote to me. If I had to choose two words to describe him, I'd pick "arms crossed." Maybe I can send a message with Mom's phone. Or talk to Jackie.

I go through the rooms, looking for my mom, Jackie, and—I guess—the captain. Everyone seems to be working. No one is in the galley. The toilet area is shut as usual. Each room is empty in a different way. Sergei and Jordan's area is sparse. Panchi and John-Michael's quarters are empty and suffering from the fire. Jackie and the captain's space is nice and neat. Our room shows that I have the messiest bunk area. And there's more stuff in there than any other room.

I find all three of them—Mom, Jackie, and the captain—on the flight deck.

They are looking down at the controls and monitors. Behind them are the four panels of windows which show a field of space with its pinpricks of light and fogs and whirls and mists. Bright reds and blues stand out.

Kepler-526, which is a reddish planet, dominates the view. On one side, it looks like it's been dipped in a fire, with swirls of darkened soot. The other, dark side looks like it's almost not even there because you can't see anything.

"Hi," I interrupt. They all look up at me and the only one smiling is my mom, who beams like she's just seen a celebrity. "Dad sent me. I mean, I have to let you guys know that my phone might be a problem. I had an issue with a blank message and he's going to wipe the device and get me a new one."

"What happened?" says the captain.

"I accidentally opened a message that Dad thinks had a virus. Then my phone started spinning."

"Take care of that first," the captain replies, looking down again.

"Do you need to use mine for something right now? I'll be working in here for a while," says my mom.

"Use that for the device inventory—did you put the list on the ship's network?" adds the captain.

"Yes," I answer. "And yes," I answer again.

Mom hands her phone to me. I start to go to the back of the ship, but Jackie stops me by talking to my mom.

"Shouldn't she work in here, in case we need that?" says Jackie.

"I can do that," I answer.

My mom says, "Sit in the co-pilot seat, please."

I slide into one of the big chairs next to the three of them and, with my mom's device, bring up the list of things to check, sorting them to see which ones haven't been accounted for and which ones still need to be inspected.

As I'm scrolling through that, Mom stops me and asks for the device back. Then Jackie says, "Andre, we're going to have to use that device, too."

Then the captain says, "Rose Marie, can we have that back? The inventory is less important than testing the navigation systems."

"Alright, cool. Thanks," I say as I push the device to my mom. "I'm going to see if I can help with the cleanup or if Dad needs something."

I go to the door and hang on the frame while I look back. Behind them, in the window panels, there's Kepler-526, in all its pink-red-grey glory. It looks like it's growing. The stars are spattered behind that—some twinkling and gleaming, some dulled by clouds of stardust.

Chapter 16

"Morning" brings a new workday and I am back in one of the work/storage rooms with a new device all set up. My dad was able to get it to me last night and it turns out I can keep working with that. Way to go, Dad. At least working keeps my mind off the feelings of embarrassment. It was so easy to hit open on that message. And I know better! I do. I do!

In fact, I would swear that it was like my thumb moved and tapped it open before I had the thought to try to delete the message. My brain knew what was happening only after I did it. Or something like that.

It happened so fast. But at the time everything slowed down, too. I am trying to shake the memory of my own thumb hitting the subject of the message. My dad said I should remember this feeling of embarrassment when someone else makes that kind of mistake because it is much easier to forgive people when you know what it feels like and you understand how these things happen.

"The good thing about it is," he said, "no one was hurt. We restored your tools, line code, and data. Think how much worse it could have been."

I think I have had enough of life lessons for a while. From not reporting the fire fast, to this? I just want to do something right for once.

And I'm sick of everyone feeling free to lecture me about stuff I already know.

Example: I don't blame myself for the fire, but I could have acted faster. Way faster. I knew it was weird and everything. I don't blame John-Michael for the fire—no one does, of course—but because it was his phone that started it, it somehow seems like it was his fault. And now Dad is finding the time to review the nuances of human error and school me about the difference between mistakes, things that look like mistakes but are really just bad things happening, and truly malicious behavior. I made a mistake. John-Michael had a crappy thing happen. And so on.

But when you get down to it, no one on this ship acts in a way that is mean or evil. The worst anyone ever does around here is ignore someone else and that can be considered self-care when you're sharing a ship with eight people and there's no way to get off of it.

My work going through all the devices has turned out to be fairly boring. Everything is accounted for. Not surprising! Where would anything go? Jordan's oobi cord was thinning, close to fraying, and might have at any moment caused a fire just like John-Michael's did. Dad is going to re-wrap it.

I look around the room at all the clear plastic sample bins with white lids and labels on them. There are three sections of bins. Two of the sections of bins hold the samples from Kepler-917 (which was rocky and dry) and Kepler-804 (which was rocky and wet). The third section holds the empty bins, waiting for Kepler-526.

You can tell from these bins that Kepler-917 and Kepler-804 each have a particular color scheme. I would call Kepler-917 a world of beige. Ecru. Yellow. Milk. Eggshell. Sand colors. Maybe some of it is as dark as rust or wood, but it's mostly a very light noodle color. Kepler-804 is a planet made of grays. Bruise colors. Blues. Blacks. Tin. Steel. Foil. Much of it is as dark as the color of the pupils of our eyes. The bins of light browns and dark grays cover two-thirds of the walls.

I take a picture. I take a couple more pictures—one from each end of the wall to show the expanse of the samples. I make it so the rocks in the bins close to me are in sharp focus and the samples in the bins behind them are very much out of focus. Then I do the reverse. Next, I switch filters and take some on infrared—these turn out to be super-boring—and some on ultraviolet—much more interesting.

Initial tests have shown Kepler-917 to have a lot of feldspar and sulfur in its make-up. That explains how its colors are so much in the yellow and light brown category. Kepler-804, on the other hand, is made of rock and water—parts of it are molten from time to time, but when (and where) we were there, it was just rock dust and water—thus the grays.

My phone lags as I'm taking pictures of the bins and samples. I think it's because of all the updates to it from loading—or I should say re-loading—code and information and tools and everything. It's about as bad as when I send images to Ethan Junior.

While all that is processing, I head to the galley to get a snack. Can't start working on an empty stomach, right?

In the galley, I take out a packet of fruit gel—raspberries and blackberries in a delicious, sugary goo. Slurp. Then some water. I am alone, so I put some blobs of water on the table, blow them around, and sip them up with a straw. Each mouthful is cool and clean-tasting. Yes, I know all the water is recycled over and over. But our recycler does a good job at making it seem perfectly filtered. And the table is very clean. And so no spiders, or whatever you Earth people have to contend with anyway.

When I was little, my mom and I used to do this. We would push water around with a straw on the galley table and imagine pictures in the tiny shapes of the water blobs skimming around. And then we would use the straw to slurp them up.

Jackie catches me in the act. "Hey, Rose Marie, what are you ..." she starts talking as she slides over next to me.

"Hey!" I respond, a little surprised, and I send a few more water blobs along onto the tabletop and catch them while she watches me.

"I'm sorry about ordering you around yesterday. About your phone. I was really focused on the nav system." Jackie looks away from the table.

"That's all right. I don't mind. It's not like an inventory breakdown could stall the ship the way a navigation system crisis could."

"I just didn't want you to feel like you weren't allowed to be there. You might be Mel and Ted's daughter, but we all care about you."

If I wasn't feeling awkward before, I do now. "Okay," I say. "I care about everyone on the ship too." Now it's my turn to look away.

Jackie smiles and starts moving toward the front of the ship. "Glad you're okay with it. I will talk to you later," she says, gliding away.

Happy to be by myself again, I wipe my hands and the table, then make my way back to our quarters to get a stylus.

Our room is in the same place, of course, but the other quarters have been reassigned because Panchi and John-Michael's area is now a melted, blackened mess. None of the air vents are functioning properly in that part of the ship, the wiring needs to be redone entirely, and it still reeks of burnt plastic. The captain is also having John-Michael and Sergei pull out all the furniture, fixtures, and equipment so we check the ship's hull in that area and test its integrity.

Panchi and John-Michael have moved to what used to be Sergei and Jordan's room. Sergei is staying there and Jordan has moved to the captain and Jackie's room. So now all the occupied quarters will have three people in each area. Ours might not be the most cluttered anymore. Then again, with me in it, our quarters probably will continue to be the most cluttered.

I'm pretty sure John-Michael and Panchi will be the most displeased. And if Sergei and Jordan are smart, they're going to have to learn to be heavy sleepers sometimes, too— if you know what I mean.

Time to head back to my work area.

I delay a little more before getting into my assignments and check my WSC account where I find I have 432 ads and junk messages. I delete everything that's not from a WSC address without opening it. That leaves me with eleven real unread messages. One of them has a weird subject line and I start to think it's some kind of trick: "Alert: your account requires maintenance." I delete that too.

Then Ethan Junior starts to ping me on chat.

hey

you were hacked buddy

How did he know what happened?

How did you know that? I opened a bad message. But my
dad caught it before it did any harm.

There's an extra pause before he responds. Space lag? Meaningful silence? It's hard to tell.

look around rosie - the infernal world - the universe is all
over you and you are all over it

And now I am starting to panic a little. I com my parents to come back here, and open a news feed. I am in seventy percent of the top headlines:

"Teenager in space"

"Rare look into life of the girl born on a spaceship"

"Scientists discuss health issues of growing up in low-g

conditions"
"How the youngest astronaut lives. Number 4 surprised me!"
"Long distance space mission hacked by rogue media outlet"
"Investigation of security at WSC because of a spaceship breach"

"Mom? Dad?" I call to my parents over the com. "I'm all over the news. I think there was more to that virus that hit my account."

My parents and Jackie arrive quickly in the workroom and take a look at my phone. They look at each other and get quiet. Then my dad springs into action. He starts his tablet and logs into his WSC account. He has almost as many unread messages as I did, but his aren't ads and news. They're WSC-security related.

My mom leaves to get her tablet and returns looking tense. "Captain's coming back here in a while to talk about this."

The three of them tune me out while they concentrate on messages from the WSC. While they do this, I scroll through my info feed. I'm sure I shouldn't open any messages or anything but reading the subjects makes me look busy. I really don't know what else to do.

Mom tells me, "Rose Marie, why don't you look around to see what's being said by the media? See how much information is being broadcast on the feed aggregators. Look for stuff that's real. Watch out. You'll see a lot of filler items with old information."

I start to read some of the posts. It looks like there isn't much, but it's spread out in a billion, billion places. These people are great at making a little information go a long way. I find myself in a slideshow that is basically five statements stretched over ten pages, each with images of generic-looking people doing things on Earth. Typical.

One post suggests I am not a human being, but an alien

with gigantic eyes, a large dome-shaped, bald head, and green skin like it's the 20th century or something.

When the captain gets to the workroom, he, Jackie, and my parents start talking about the situation, if any classified information got released, and if the ship's network, navigation software, or environmental controls were compromised. First of all, there isn't really that much that's classified on the Grimm Explorer. So much information about it has already been in the news and posted by WSC for promotional purposes. If you've seen the WSC sites and channels, you already know what I'm talking about.

Mom and Dad have two main worries. One is about me and my privacy. The other is about the integrity of everything electronic—from the programming to the oobi ports—on the ship. Jackie chimes in, "Do you think someone hostile could take over any of our functions remotely from Earth?"

The captain starts issuing orders, one to each of us. "Mel, you put together a statement for WSC to give to the media indicating that while there was a breach of security, we are safe and there isn't any new information to release. Add to that a plea for folks to respect Rosie's privacy. Say it nicer than that."

Mom gives the captain a half-grin and gives me a look while he continues his list.

"Ted, I know you're already working on systems checks, but I want you to look at Rosie's old phone again and the new, re-imaged phone. Maybe virus tools are running in the background. Jackie, start a second diagnostic on the navigation software and our coordinate tracking. I want to make sure we are where we're supposed to be and we're going where we're supposed to be going."

At this point I'm anxious, am I now going to be in the roll call of orders? Am I? Yes. It's my turn.

"Rosie, I'm going to contact Ethan O'Neil—senior—and have him get WSC to set you up with something else. That will get you a new user id for chat and a new system account. You need to change all your social locations, too, wherever they might be. That will limit the number of people who know how to contact you directly."

My dad says, "That's not going to fix anything."

The captain responds, "Sure, but it might prevent something else from happening. Rose Marie, if Ethan O'Neil tells you to take any particular actions, be sure to follow those instructions, you hear me?"

"Yes, sir," I tell him.

"I think we're done here," says the captain. "Each of you, message a status update to me at the end of the day."

I take a deep breath. This is going to put everything on hold for a while. School, vid projects, assignments, and keeping up with Ethan Junior. It's like breaking my toe. I started out intending all kinds of things to do and see, then I end up getting sidelined by something unexpected.

Chapter 17

My parents have banished anything that connects me to the Earth for a while. So I'm in the burnt room without any devices.

We've had to change and clean the air filters five times in the one day since the fire. John-Michael and Sergei have done most of the actual work. They've scraped off the burnt plastic, torn out the melted bunks, broken down the materials and equipment that we think can't be used again.

Some of the back rooms hold leftover bits and pieces from the fire. The mindset on the ship is to reuse as much as possible, but the instinct is to keep everything as tidy as possible. Added together, it means the burnt stuff is stacked, labeled, and set aside. We jettison very little around here.

I spend time wiping down everything, but it looks as if this area of the ship is now going to be more like a hallway— my first hallway. Since it's in the middle of our quarters, we can only use it for a little bit of storage. I know a couple home improvement vid channels that would tell us how to make bookcases or sets of drawers to line the sides of this part of the ship to make a useful and tasteful space with a 2080s look and feel.

But I like it the way it is now, all scorched and barren. Once I get a hold of my devices again—if I ever get a hold of my devices again—I might want to use it to make a vid with a burnt-out background. I'll call it "The Planet of Doom" and just have snakes sliding around catching lizards and cats and chickens and such. No dialog. Dramatic music. The thrill of the chase. Something like that.

I think Ethan Junior could use that kind of vid. I'm sure he needs more material for our channel (which is more his channel, to be honest).

But first, I need to figure out if my parents will trust me again or—if I can't get that trust back—if they will let me slide back into my old privileges so I can make a vid and send it to Ethan Junior. Note: They are not the kind of people who forget easily or let things slide.

Besides, their trust is what I really want. I feel incredibly embarrassed that all of this happened. I want to move on from this as fast as possible.

This is what I'm thinking about while I pack up my cleaning materials when Jordan comes through.

"Hey, Rose Marie," Jordan calls out.

"Hey," I answer.

"You're on clean-up duty?"

"Yeah, and I have no devices. That is possibly the most difficult part."

"Have you talked to your mom and dad about getting them back? You'd be surprised at how far a simple and earnest request will go with adults."

I answer him with silence because that seems like an awkward conversation with the parental crew members.

Jordan continues, "Alright. I know it'll be much easier than you think because your situation is more about having time to check and clear the devices than it is about punishing you. So I'll go check with them. And, between you and me, it's more convenient for everyone, not just you, for you to be connected and up and available."

"Thank you," I say. "It's a little thing, but I have this idea for a vid and it's making me feel anxious about not getting to do it."

Jordan sits down on the floor. He is possibly the only person on the ship who can look relaxed sitting on the floor among cleaning supplies and burnt up walls.

"Yeah? What's the idea of the vid?"

I think he is settling in. "Oh, I, uh, don't like to talk about it till it's done. I, um, feel like the idea gets emptied out if I talk about it. But, if I don't talk about it, it seems like the idea simmers, or grows like a bacteria culture in the lab or something. And sometimes the idea changes as I make the vid."

"So I'm not going to hear this idea? Even if I promise not to hold you to it?"

"That's the less important part of it. It's more about no one seeing it. I can make and break things without anyone seeing it."

"What do you do with the vids?"

"I send the good ones to Ethan Junior—there have been about four and a half good ones. And he puts them on our channel."

"Hey, that is great! Can I see the vids? What's the channel name?"

"I don't think you would like them." I start to squirm, like I just told him, I don't want people looking over my shoulder. These vids are not THAT great. And I'm playing around half the time. So is Ethan Junior.

Jordan smiles. "Ah. I can see by the panic in your face that you do not want to share that information. Sure. Sure, that's cool. I'm not trying to make an intractive study of you. I will lay off. But if you ever do want someone in the audience who is probably a little too interested in your work because he thinks of himself as an uncle or something, let me know."

I remain silent. There's really nothing to say.

Jordan gets up and says, "Well, alright. I'll tell your parents to come talk to you about finishing up the device check quickly. You have things to do and vids to make."

Jordan continues his path through the area. I wonder how long it will take my mom or dad to arrive. Ten seconds? Five? How long does it take your family to find you in a house or something? Must be like a full minute or something.

I am tempted to start a timer, but since I have no phone, I can't do that.

Both of my parents find me before I'm done putting away the cleaning supplies.

Mom starts the discussion. "Jordan talked to us."

"We're not punishing you, you know," Dad chimes in.

"Okay." This is my brilliant contribution to the conversation.

"It's a little bit of a punishment," Mom corrects Dad. "We want to make sure you understand the consequences of a security lapse on a ship like this with corporate, military, and governmental missions."

"We will have the most problems with the corporate interests," says Dad. "They have the money."

"Ted, don't get into that." Mom sometimes shuts down any geo-political-financial-legal-big-business talk that is sent in my direction from Dad and I am a little bit glad about that. Adults do go on and on about that stuff. It all makes me nervous.

"All right, Mel," Dad answers. "But, Rosie, honey, you will get the devices and access back as soon as we can. First of all, it wasn't totally your fault. Second, people make these kinds of mistakes all the time. But you better be aware that if there's any real serious trouble, there will be more lectures and deep discussions and serious talks about digital security than you can stand. And I promise it will be both terrible and boring."

"Thanks," I answer. "I mean thanks for trying to get me a phone or something back—not for the promise of terrible and boring lectures."

Chapter 18

None of this—the fire, the clean-up of the fire, checking all the systems on the ship, the virus (or hack), or checking all the systems on the ship again—none of it has changed the fact that we are going to arrive at Kepler-526 in another day.

When we get there, there's a tight schedule for completing everything involved in going down to the planet and back up again four times (once with drones, once with robots, twice with crew) and then getting the ship flying back toward Earth.

When we get to Kepler-526, we'll do the same things we did at Kepler-917 (the beige planet) and at Kepler-804 (the gray planet). We first send drones to scope out the situation. The drones do a fly-by, take pictures, sample the atmosphere, and test weather-related factors. The next step is to send down robots. They land, roll around, and do what the drones did, but on the surface of the planets.

After the drones and the robots, Mom and Jackie made the two trips to the surface of Kepler-917. At Kepler-804, Sergei also went with Mom and Jackie for both of the manned landings. Because of the water on Kepler-804, they wanted to take more samples and so needed more people to do the work. Plus they were worried about the equipment functioning—or rather not functioning—on the surface of Kepler-804. That made it a good time to have an onsite backup crew.

Everyone on the ship has been trained in the procedures for planet walking. But both trips to Kepler-526 are going to be left in Mom and Jackie's hands because of the way the planet rotates and because they are by far the most qualified pilots.

Did you notice how I said *everyone* on the ship has been trained in the procedures for planet walking? That includes me. Yes! My whole life has been about maintaining procedures for safety. But, also, yes, the main reason this ship is out here with us on it, is to see if we can hit these Goldilocks planets and find out more about them in person and collect actual samples. So I have gotten to go through all the vid training, testing, mock runs, simulations, and certification courses that they have available.

The nice thing about Kepler-526 is that it has about half Earth's gravity—which is double the gravity level on the ship. Yes, I know there are risks, but they do not seem like big risks. I mean it's only half Earth gravity, right? How hard could it be?

When I ask my mom about getting to step foot on the surface of Kepler-526, she tilts her head and hums a little, "Mmmmm, maybe."

Maybe. Maybe. Maybe.

Hope. Hope. Hope.

Chapter 19

If they are going to name any planet after me, it's this one. I know they won't do any such thing, but this is the planet that is just like my life. Think about it: there is a small space for human survival. A little bit wrong in either direction, and it means it's not going to happen. The flying is critical.

What? You think it's not just like my life? Well, okay, it's not just like my life, but it might be the first planet I get to stand on and it's a better metaphor than the noodle-colored planet is, that's all I have to say.

Plus, it's where I'm at right now. We've hit the planet at the appointed time in spite of everything and we're currently orbiting it. FLT flight is off. The ship no longer hums. In about two hours, it'll be time to send down the drones. When they come back, we'll send down the robots.

The ship is busy. The crew is totally taken up with pre-flight planning and checking for the drones. Like I said, I'm shadowing Mom and Jackie for this. They think it will be good for me to know what goes into it, especially if I'm ever going to get out of the spaceship myself

So they are working and I'm watching them. Mom talks through everything she does, narrator-style. Jackie sort of talks through what she does, but when she's working, she starts more sentences than she finishes:

"Here I'm setting the schedule for the..."

"With the flight plan in..."

"Before we can engage the system process for moving..."

Then she gets quiet and intense while she does the things that would have ended her sentences.

I stay next to my mom. She is going through the plans with me as she checks everything against the new data we're receiving, now that we're right here orbiting the planet.

"This always happens," Mom says. "The information about wind and local weather changes our plans. It's completely expected, though. Here, I'll show you how this means we have to adjust the launch direction coordinates for the drones."

I watch how she runs an algorithm for airspeed velocity and flight patterns.

"It's nice to have the computer run this process through, isn't it?"

She's talking about some of the school projects I've had where I simulate parts of the automatic process with manual calculations. Yes, I would agree with her. It is nice to have software handle all of it. But I am secretly also glad to know how all the math behind it works and to have done that by hand. It can be an elegant and slow way to think about what's happening right now, practically instantaneously. And if I minded doing anything one manual step at a time, I would not be making stop-motion films with foil-covered styluses and a phone camera.

Over the next ninety minutes, we continue our work. Or rather, they continue to work and to talk through (or partly talk through) the setup and launch sequences. I watch, feeling jumpy, sometimes asking questions. It's getting close to the lift-off time.

Then Mom says, "Rose Marie, we're going to do the first manned flight without you. I think you've already figured that out. It's a bit of tricky flying and we don't want any extra weight. Can you understand that? I know you were looking forward to it."

"Sure, Mom," I answer, feeling a little disappointed.

"We are, however, much more serious about your going down on the second manned flight to Kepler-526. We'll have already navigated it. We might even have you and Jackie go without me. It would be a great chance for you get to experience more substantial amounts of gravity."

"Okay, Mom." I am relieved, disappointed, excited, and anxious all at once. It will be so much easier to stay on the ship. And this postpones the moment where I have to go out onto a planet. Yep, the feeling includes relief, disappointment, excitement, and anxiety, but I still get to be hopeful about the possibility of going down to the planet later. I have all the emotions.

They send me through the ship to bring over anyone interested in the drone launch. I go back through our tube-like ship, interrupting work and conversations with the reminder to go watch the launch from the flight deck or back near the launch bay. Other than birthday dinners and the occasional all-crew meeting, this is one of the few times we gather together to do the same thing at the same time. They could have sent a com message.

Only Panchi plans to miss this one. When I talk to her, she responds, but doesn't look up from her work. (Of course.) Everyone else wants to be on the flight deck where the biggest windows are.

Sometimes—like now—I feel like a mascot. But what I'm doing is also a task I know how to do and I am happy to do it. Sometimes I like doing something that is not hard or new for once. I can be a mascot with confidence, as I have spent so much time being one up until this point in my life.

Everyone on the flight deck is standing. Mom and

Jackie are huddled with their work. Sergei leans against the bulkhead.

Jordan nudges Sergei when he comes in. "Did I miss anything?" he asks.

"Not yet," Sergei says.

"Ha ha," replies Jordan, sarcastically. He winks at me. (How much of a little kid do I seem to him?)

My dad hovers near me and I'm playing it cool, trying to do the same kind of nonchalant leaning that Sergei is doing. But I do not think that I am pulling it off because my shoulder slips against the bulkhead a lot.

John-Michael stands by himself, watching the planet in the big windows. John-Michael has the least business-like way of looking at things. He looks kind of star-struck. I get to say that phrase literally, I guess, out here among the stars. The captain watches the windows, too, but he does it in his arms-crossed kind of way.

Dad monitors the connection with the WSC. He looks focused and bored simultaneously. Sergei stays at the ship's controls for the drone launch.

Do we have a countdown like in the old movies? Yes. It makes for a nice ceremony. And it helps when I'm timing my picture taking. Which, by the way, I am allowed to do so long as it doesn't interfere with anything.

We also play music. It is Jordan's turn to pick the music and he has chosen a song from like 150 years ago. It's called "Flash" by Queen. The lyrics are about a superhero of some kind saving Earth and it has a lot of people talking in it, but I like the clear voice of the main singer. I had been expecting classical music or jazz—because it is Jordan, after all.

The four drones fly out like mosquitos from the ship and swoop toward Kepler-526. The data stream runs in real-time collecting flight data, temperature data, wind data, light data. You know: data.

The drones have about four hours of flight time. My

mom continues to be concerned about wind speeds. Jackie reaffirms that it's okay, "They are within the projected range."

"Right. But I am allowed to think we have to be careful," says my mom.

"Yep. I think we are always allowed to think that," replies Jackie with a smile.

Jordan is the first to leave the flight deck. Mumbling about work to do, he heads toward the back of the ship. John-Michael follows him, but I know he's probably going to go looking for Panchi. The two of them will be heads-down over their individual work for the rest of the day, but they'll be heads-down over their individual work together.

My dad sits in the co-pilot chair and stares out the windows. The drones are far enough away that they're hard to see. Then he looks to his tablet and checks each of the systems to make sure everything is working fine. During all the flights, even the drone and robot flights, that's what my dad focuses on: status checks.

"You don't have to stay, Rose Marie," Dad says.

"I know, but I want to," I respond. "It's the only live action drama I ever get."

"What? You mean getting to watch me and Mom sew is not enough for you? All right," Dad's face turns a little pink and he turns to the captain. "Are we going to delay the robots at all?"

"No," says the captain, who turns and leaves the flight deck.

"Do you think there are any issues that would delay the robots, Melissa?" Dad asks Mom.

"Nope. I still think the wind speeds are a concern," replies my mom. Jackie throws her a look. "I do!" Mom says in Jackie's direction. "But there's nothing that would indicate that we should change any plans."

"All right then," replies Dad. "I'll be back in a few hours when the drones come back, to help with the robot launch."

And I am staying right here with my phone, looking out at this rusty planet, waiting on drones and robots, listening to my mom and Jackie joke about wind speed, storms, flight patterns, and landing plans.

Chapter 20

The drones zip back like drunk mosquitoes in a vid—a little slower and a little shaky as they hum into the launch bay and attach themselves to the docking rings. Then Jackie taps the button to make the extension arms pull them back into the launch bay.

The two robots are set up to go next. Unlike the nameless drones, we have dubbed the robots Itchy and Scratchy. Itchy and Scratchy will be controlled manually, one each by Mom and Jackie. Mom gets Itchy, I think, and Jackie gets Scratchy. The robots are much bigger than the drones.

We seal the launch bay and Sergei, Panchi, and John-Michael go in there to prepare the robots. This process also gives Mom and Jackie a little bit of down-time before the next phase of our visit.

At 2300 hours, the robots are ready and Mom and Jackie are back on the flight deck with me, Dad, Sergei, and the captain. Sergei activates their launch with the push of a button. Then we shift our attention to Mom and Jackie.

The captain stands behind Jackie and touches her shoulder while she and my mom focus on the robots. If it weren't for the background of the planet's horizon and the space behind that, this would seem like a tense gaming session.

Jackie puts her hand over her husband's when the robots hit the ground. Mom looks up and around the room, doing a mental inventory of her family. We are both here, grinning at her.

When I was little, I used to ask my parents if they were good at their jobs and they would kind of skirt the question or answer for the other one: yes, your mom/dad is very good at their job or we would not be here right now. Now that I'm older, I think I can make that assessment myself. And right now I think: yes, my mom is very good at her job, or that robot would not be sitting in exactly the right place right now.

The robots need more monitoring and their trip will last longer than the drones' trip. But I have been in the flight deck for many hours already and so I go back to my bunk to catch a nap or chat with Ethan Junior. Both probably.

My mom stops me before I leave the room, "Ah, hang on—are you going to want to be up for the first manned flight? It's at 0600 hours."

"Yes," I reply.

"Okay. I'll join you soon. I need to get some rest, too. I get the first 'off' shift."

Then Mom hits her tablet and contacts Sergei and John-Michael. "Sergei? John-Michael? Can you come up to the flight deck? I want to start the shift change. And tell Panchi the samples will be coming in from the robots soon. On schedule."

I am already in my bunk in my sleeping clothes, under my blanket, when my mom moves into our quarters. Of course, I have my phone in the bunk with me and I'm messaging Ethan Junior with some of the pictures I took of the drones leaving the ship. I close my eyes during the lags, but I'm not going to fall asleep yet.

Mom slides into the room and comes up to my bunk. "I'm sure tomorrow will be great," she starts. She moves her hand to my forehead and traces the edge of my hair, where there are some fine baby hairs. I reach out my hand and she joins hers to mine in a slow handshake.

"Mm," I answer, feeling like this is a good night. It's exciting, sure, but Mom and Jackie have done this smoothly a couple times before. It's almost routine.

Chapter 21

When I wake up, I think I've slept too long. Mom's already out of our quarters. It seems too quiet where I am—and not just because we are no longer at FTL speed. I undo the straps and get out of my bunk. Then I put the blanket away, shoving it into my locker. No, it is not folded.

I pull on a clean jumpsuit and head back to the galley for something to eat, checking the food schedule on my phone first.

I am slurping up water from a container and getting a fruit gel when my phone pops off. The all-com has been activated and it's my mom, talking to Sergei at the command center. She probably should have made that a two-way com. But at least now I know she and Jackie are already on their way down to Kepler-526. I squeeze the rest of the gel into my mouth, the sweet mixing together with the water. I thought she was going to wake me for the flight.

Mom is talking about a storm. "It's not as bad as I thought it was going to be," she relays to Sergei. I wish I'd seen the launch from the ship, but I'll get to see them dock on the way back. I can ask her then why she didn't come get me when she gets back. She was probably too busy and I was asleep.

I cycle down the volume on my phone.

Before I head to the front of the ship, I go back to see what's going on with the samples from the robots. Panchi and John-Michael are sorting, cataloging, and storing them. The wall has a new, small-for-now section of containers that have reddish rocks in them. Rust. Brown. Orange. Raspberry. Copper.

"Are there a lot of new samples?" I ask.

Panchi answers without looking at me, "The usual amount that we get from Itchy and Scratchy." Then she pauses, looks at me, then looks at the ceiling. "Yes, it's the usual amount."

"Ah," I say, not really knowing how to answer. I think I'm intruding on their conversation. But before I leave, I take a picture of the two of them, heads bowed over the steel table with the samples, some empty (or half-empty) plastic containers in front of them, some filled containers stacked behind them.

That's a good one, I think, and I send it to Ethan Junior without comment. My phone spins, pauses, and then I receive a picture of his backyard with its green, green, green, green, green grass. Vast amounts of green grass are laid out for about 30 meters behind his family's house. I must have a green deficiency because it seems so bright. There is a soccer goal in the frame which I know for a fact he doesn't use at all. The used-to-be-white netting looks grayish (from sitting in the sun and rain and a few hurricanes and floods?). The sunlight in the yard makes everything seem drenched in a slightly yellow gloss, like a lightbulb reflection in copper wiring. The light on the ship is white all the time.

I'm scooting to the front of the ship again, through the galley, toilet and shower, and the four sets of quarters. I'll probably spend the rest of the first manned flight trying to stay out of the way. When I get to our quarters, I load up a book to read and lie back in my bunk.

I turn the sound on my phone up and mute the com so I can listen to the flight chatter. Jackie is telling my mom that they have collected enough.

My mom says, "Good. It's time to get out of here. Wind velocity is picking up."

They continue to go back and forth talking about each item left on their checklist for the planet walk and eventual lift-off. I tap through the book, not paying much attention to them. Their banter is background noise.

When they've finished gathering some of the samples and they've loaded them in Little Bear, my mother and Jackie decide to move the shuttle to the second location to get another batch of samples during this run.

They gently get the small shuttle lifted and start to maneuver it to the second location. I close the book tool and get out of the bunk.

It is a short glide from our quarters to the flight deck and as I'm moving through the forward-most doorway to the flight deck, the far-away shuttle surges and rolls. It rolls in an impossible way, into the dark side of the planet. The alarm on the shuttle monitor starts blaring as the temperature gauge drops and the darkness swallows Little Bear.

And then the alarm turns off. All of the sounds from Little Bear are quiet. My ears are full of this silence. Then Dad hits the ship's communication button and yells at it: "Melissa!" He pulls his phone out and shakes it, pushes on the phone's com and yells again: "Melissa!"

Everyone has pushed into the flight deck while Dad works the communications. My face is really close to my dad's back and I think I need to just concentrate on the weave and grain of the fabric of his clothes. Sergei tries activating the remote control of the vessel. Captain orders Jordan to prepare for injuries. Jordan says it'll be cold-related and crash-related injuries. He adds that he has the materials with the medical supplies.

I think I'm going to throw up, the taste of that sweet fruit gel is in my teeth and I hate it.

Sergei establishes control over the shuttle, and we can see him navigate it back on course. He looks like he's not aware of anything else—his face is a flat metal wall except for his shifting eyes.

Dad continues to try to raise any communication with Mom and Jackie. I pull out my phone and look at the recent thread with my mom. The last thing she wrote to me was, "Are you in the sample area?" That was yesterday.

I send a message: "Mom." But the message is outlined in red: it's not delivered. I send another message: "Hello?" It's not delivered either. I shut off the device and restart it.

Panchi and John-Michael leave to go to the launch bay.

The captain and I watch Sergei and my dad work.

My dad has gotten Little Bear on an oobi connect with his device and synced those two with the ship, but there are no human responses.

Sergei manually navigates the shuttle all the way to the docking rings which he uses to pull it into the launch bay. The captain tells my dad to stay on the flight deck. "Keep working on maintaining the shuttle-ship connection. Make sure we have all the data," he says and his eyes skip over to me. "You stay here, too. Help your dad."

Panchi and John-Michael are processing the shuttle now that it's been secured in the launch bay and the captain and Jordan leave to help with them. Sergei is still at the flight deck controls so he can handle the shuttle remotely. My dad and I watch the planet and our screens, but we do not look at each other.

Eventually, Dad stands up and takes my right hand in both of his. He looks in my eyes and says, "Let's see what's going on with shuttle."

Chapter 22

Except for dents on the outside and a broken environmental system, Little Bear is not damaged. They pulled the bodies of my mother and her friend from the cockpit. A temporarily broken environmental system was all that needed to happen to kill them.

The data from their suits indicated that they were alive when Little Bear rolled into the dark side of the planet, but that rolling damaged the part of the system that kept the shuttle warm enough. They froze to death very quickly. Were frozen. Very fast.

Most of the time, access to the launch bay is restricted because it's shut off from the ship's environmental system to save energy. It can be used as an airlock if we need to use it that way, but there's no reason to support it continuously.

For the rest of the mission, the plan is for my mother and Jackie's bodies to be stored there. I guess I could make a point about how it's appropriate because of their love of space and piloting. But I don't really see any meaning here. It's going to be a storage unit for them. A big metal body bag.

I'm glad it's usually locked off. Otherwise, I'd want to go out there, I think. This way, I can't.

Chapter 23

Jordan has not let me see her body and it does not feel real. I don't believe any of this happened. I know I saw the shuttle roll over, but it looked like a toy. It looked like something you see on a vid for selling toys or a vid of planes doing tricks at an air show on Earth.

Sergei has been working on Little Bear. He found a piece of equipment in the environmental system that cracked. This was enough to have taken the whole thing out. One piece. It was one of the conductors. After he replaced it, the environmental system came up and worked again like nothing had happened.

The captain says we're still going to send another group down for the second manned flight. He says that anything else would be a waste of the work my mom and Jackie did. Sergei is the next best pilot. The captain also says Sergei should be the one to do most of the work, but that the next most knowledgeable pilot is me. I know my mom and Jackie already trained me and planned for me to go on this trip. Mom even made that space suit for me. I should go, he says.

A week ago, I was freaking out over an inventory of devices. This week, everything has changed. In some kind of weird eye-blink, I lost my mother and I am dealing with going to walk on an uninhabited planet—not that I have ever walked on an inhabited planet before.

Also, the captain has asked us to create a plan to launch in the next 24 hours. Any more time and the position of the planet and our orbit around it would no longer be at an optimal range for continuing back to Earth, and we'd have to hang out here for a few Earth-months to get back into that range. Sergei assures me that we can base our plan on the procedures and calculations my mom and Jackie already outlined for this. There wouldn't be too much to change.

I really don't know how the others are so calm and decided. My head is full of static. I am barely able to think about anything. And I'm baffled that the captain thinks I should still go through with it even though neither my mom nor Jackie are here. I know I worked with them when they were developing the flight plans and mechanics of the flight. I did. But still, most of the time, I'm trying to keep myself from going to my bunk and hiding under my blanket.

Maybe I'm just the most expendable person. Maybe they think losing me would not be a great tragedy. I'm extraneous anyway. It's not just about assessing my abilities and putting me in a situation with a higher gravity, is it? What are they thinking?

Chapter 24

John-Michael asked everyone to come to the galley at 1800 hours for a memorial. I don't want to go, but my dad says I have to. And it's not like I can escape or anything on this ship.

When I get there, Panchi and John-Michael are talking and Panchi is putting her phone inside her jumpsuit. Maybe she's going to pay attention for once.

I try to make my already-undersized body even smaller through force of will. My dad arrives and nudges against me, shoulder to shoulder. We are two people with a seam between us. His warmth is different than my mom's, but it is like a word that rhymes with her warmth. And I need it.

After Jordan, Sergei, and the captain join us, John-Michael says we're going to honor our fallen family and friends as much as possible.

"Let's begin with a moment of silence," he says.

All the others bow their heads. I don't. I look at each face and try to study their expressions, which, by the way, seem mostly blank. There are two exceptions. My dad looks like he is physically sick like he's going to throw up. The captain looks like a robot. His face is stiff. His eyes remain open as he looks downward, so you can't really see them.

John-Michael is the first to speak. "They say death is nothing. That our loved ones are just in the next room. They say that everything we had, remains; that everything we had between us, remains and can never die. We should not be sorry, they say. We should be happy for having been in each other's lives."

"They say that once love has been created, it never fades. Melissa and Jack created so much love in their lives, with their family and friends, with everyone on this ship. I am sure that is eternal. That will never be lost."

"Would anyone like to share?" he asks. "Andre? Ted?"

Now I am the one with my head bowed. The tears are pulling down from my eyes. I wipe them into my hair and there are more tears. They fall as I move my head, shaking it side to side. Some of them get in my mouth. The taste is clear and salty, too.

I hear my shipmates' voices, but I don't know what they're saying. It doesn't last long. I think no one has really accepted anything.

"I can't," my dad chokes out.

And the captain says nothing.

John-Michael brings this event to a close. He says, "We have never tried to name any of the Kepler planets that we visited. But now, I think Keplerr-526 should become Finch-Hernandez. It will be a permanent memorial to these amazing people who were the first long-distance space pilots and our friends, our wives, our mom."

So this is how we'll name the planets. For what we lose.

Chapter 25

The bodies of my mother and Jackie are washed, dressed, and wrapped in their fireproof blankets. Then they are zipped into black body bags. Yes, there have been body bags on the ship this whole time.

Jordan and John-Michael take the bodies to the launch bay. The bodies then get strapped into containers along the wall on the left side where they will remain and will stay frozen until we get back to Earth. Don't worry, the launch bay doors will be shut so the bodies won't burn up on re-entry.

At the memorial, John-Michael said it was like they were just in the next room. Keeping their bodies this way means they are, you know, physically and literally, in the next room. But *they* aren't.

I know what I am supposed to believe. I saw the body bags. It did not feel like my mother was in one of them. She is gone, and the figure in the bag could have been made of rubber, spray foam, and paper cardboard. It had nothing to do with anything, and it certainly had nothing to do with me.

Chapter 26

Sergei and I are on the flight deck. He and I are, again, stepping each other through the plan and calculations my mom and Jackie made.

The plan looks like a trip down and back with no additional side trips while we are on the planet. No second location. We can follow what they had almost exactly, though the plans have been adjusted a little since Mom and Jackie did them. I like the idea of following a path that Mom made, it's an impression. I wish I could walk it with her.

The captain comes into the flight deck and folds his arms across his chest. He asks, "Ready in three hours?"

Sergei does the talking, "Yes."

"Will Rosie be ready?"

Sergei looks at me. "She's got her skills and training. Rosie? Do you want to go? Are you ready?"

I am sure I am supposed to say something confident like "Can do!" or "I've got this." But instead, I blurt out, "I think I can if I'm not alone."

What I mean is that I can do it if Sergei is there and my

dad takes care of the systems from the ship and the captain watches from the flight deck and Panchi and John-Michael monitor the process, and I trace the path my mother and Jackie made. But I think I also mean that I need somehow not to feel abandoned by my mom. That is a gross thought. I know it's not right. But my mother is gone and it seems like she took herself away and that is not fair to me.

The captain nods.

Sergei and I close what we're working on and go to check on our spacesuits for the planet walk.

On board the ship, we have eight spacesuits (one for each member of the original crew). The two that were designed for and used by my mom and Jackie were salvaged. It is unlikely that anyone is ever going to use those. I'm using the one made for Jordan that was altered to fit me. Sergei can still use his own suit, the one he used back on Kepler-804.

After this trip, we won't need any more space suits, I don't think—not unless we have to go out of the ship to repair it while in orbit or something.

My spacesuit is loose, even with all the changes. I feel like a joke. I've stuffed padding into them, but my feet still slip around inside Panchi's size-9 boots. We were able to switch out Panchi's boots for Jordan's because they're smaller, but still, you can't really alter those. Panchi comes and helps check the stitching and joints while I'm trying it on. When we're done, just as I'm about to take off the suit, Panchi holds my shoulders in her hands. She looks me in the eyes through the glass faceplate and says, "You are loved. You are cared for." Then she looks down and away and quickly turns and leaves before I can get the helmet off or say anything back. My throat is raw from feeling things. My body is sore, too.

It's probably good I couldn't say anything because I don't know how to respond.

Chapter 27

Sergei and I are strapped into Little Bear. We go through the checklist. We go through the countdown. It's all like a dream.

John-Michael and Sergei have triple-checked the machinery on the shuttle, from the environmental system to the docking hydraulics.

The launch bay seems just wide enough for Little Bear, so when the door rolls up, the view of the planet from the pilot seats is the biggest view of anything I have ever seen. It should be just like looking at it from the flight deck, but it's not. There's no frame to it.

The arms with the docking rings push Little Bear out of its bay. When the shuttle latches release the clasps, the vehicle shifts with a creak and a bang. Sergei activates the piloting system and we slip free of the ship.

I mean we are really free of the ship, loose out in the atmosphere of the planet attached to absolutely nothing. Little Bear arcs down toward the spot Mom and Jackie identified for the third set of samples. We are too far away from the second location to go back near where they died.

Good thing. I might want to crawl over to there and bury myself.

It is an hour flight, and everything proceeds as planned except my father has made sure to talk to us the whole time, his voice a tether between Little Bear and the Grimm Explorer. He has me repeat the readouts back to him and it keeps me focused on processing what they mean.

Maybe the air in Little Bear is especially dry. My throat is scratchy and has started to feel sore. My skin feels hot, too. Everything seems heavy. I'm sure it is all from all of the stress and gravity.

In front of us is the big, red, pink, mauve planet getting bigger and bigger. Now there is no horizon, only planet. In spite of all the work and coordination, my body tells my brain we are about to crash. Except we don't crash, we make our way along our trajectory with no bumps. There's almost no wind. The storm that Mom was so worried about has vanished.

Sergei makes Little Bear hover for a moment—as if for the dramatic effect of it—and then we land, the feet of the shuttle firmly stuck to the ground.

We pick up the equipment. I push the switch for the door. And, without even the same amount of ceremony we had for the shuttle landing, I am on the ground. Feet down.

I feel like I have weights on my feet and hands and head. My face and mouth and lips pull downward. I am three point five million, billion, zillion times heavier now. Does this explain the sweat that now covers my skin? I have never felt this slippery.

Sergei is doing the sample collecting because I'm mostly dealing with being upright. And dizzy.

Sergei comes toward me, stumbles once, realigns himself. He looks at my face through the faceplate, uses the inter-suit communication system and asks—a little slurred (maybe his tongue feels funny too)—"Are you alright?"

"I'm okay," I say. The words flop out of my mouth, which

only seems to be able to approximate the shapes that they usually make. "I am here on the ground. On a planet. I am okay." I smile—but I know he can't see very well through the visor, so I nod my head to underscore the feeling.

"We're going back soon. You walk around some. And then why don't you get back into Little Bear?"

That sounds like a good plan. I haul my legs for exactly five steps away from the shuttle ladder and then back. Then I do it again, straining against the pull of gravity. Maybe I should use my hands to lift and drop my thighs? I climb with my monstrously gigantic body up the ladder and back into Little Bear, where I shift myself into the co-pilot seat and strap myself down, exhausted.

Sergei stacks the second set of samples in the back of the shuttle and installs himself in his seat.

We run the checklist. I am feeling detached from it and glad that we have such a strict process to go through.

Dad has been monitoring us and opens the communication link again. He and Sergei initiate the takeoff. The shuttle jumps off the ground and Sergei has me take over and hover Little Bear for a moment. Gravity pulls on us. Then our blasters tear us off the planet and throw us toward the Grimm Explorer.

Finch-Hernandez—the first planet where I ever walked, the planet that memorializes my mom and her friend—recedes. I look at it through the monitor and try to shove the sight of it in my brain so I can have it there forever. One side is hidden in shadow. One side is bright with light from its sun. It looks like it was dipped into paints on that side. It would be too easy to call it a metaphor for my emotions, so I won't. Instead, I clench my teeth together very hard.

We open our suits by undoing the helmets and pulling them off. The air in the shuttle is sweet compared to what the air in a suit gets to be after even a short time. I can't shake this tired feeling. The higher gravity was all-encompassing and felt like blankets enveloping my entire body, including my earlobes. (I have never been so aware of my earlobes!) My blood seems to be pooled in my legs. I still feel it in my bones and limbs.

Sergei's face is very tense and he tells me to close my eyes.

"I'm okay," I tell him.

"I don't know, malyshka. You now look greenish."

Getting Little Bear locked back into the launch bay requires flying close to the ship. The ship extends the large docking rings that latch onto the shuttle. When the shuttle and the ship are engaged, and all the connecting components fit together, the docking rings retract into the ship, bringing the shuttle with it.

Since the bay serves as an airlock, once we're in it, we stay there. It takes about five minutes for everything to be pressurized.

I don't think it's normal—maybe it is—but I'm feeling very cold and very hot, alternately. My eyes hurt so much that I ask Sergei if his eyes hurt.

Sergei says, "No. Rose Marie. You look terrible. You must feel sick. Like I said, your face—very pale, kind of green."

"That's not part of this?" I respond. "That's not gravity? I thought the changes in atmospheric pressure were making my body ache. You don't feel this?"

"No, Rose Marie. You're sick. After we finish docking, I will get Jordan. Muscle aches from gravity will happen tomorrow, and not like this."

My eyelids drop closed then. I'm fading into sleep right here in my seat in Little Bear.

Chapter 28

When the shuttle door opens with a whoosh about ten minutes later, I wake, but I keep my eyes closed and listen. Sergei is talking to Jordan from inside the shuttle, so I peel my lids open. He has already unbuckled himself.

"Hi," I say.

"Oh, good," says Sergei, who starts to exit. "You stay here."

In the launch bay, Sergei calls out for the others.

"Ted! Jordan!" he yells. "Rose Marie became sick during our return flight. I don't know what with—or how. Don't know."

I think I can rest my eyes again. Yes?

Next thing I know my dad is in Little Bear and undoing the latches on my seat. I hold onto his arms and he pulls me to our quarters, hands under my armpits while I try my best to move my legs along the ground and tell him what happened.

"It's all right," Dad says. "I've got you. It'll be okay."

He's got a container of water and puts the tube in my mouth. The water rinses in. A drop escapes at the corner of my lips and dribbles down my chin. My eyes cross trying to look at it.

"Oh, honey," Dad says, his hand on my forehead. "You have a very high fever."

Jordan pushes next to him and presses a sensor to my skin. "Thirty-nine-point-one. Ted, get some ice."

Jordan's voice seems far away. "We're going to see if we can let this take its course. If there's a bacterial infection, we'll try some adaptive antibiotics."

Dad sounds tense. "How could this happen? What would make her sick? I don't understand."

That's the last thing I'm aware of for a long time. When I finally wake up, the room is mostly dark and I have a damp cloth in my hand. I pull the blanket over my shoulder. This is the grossest feeling I've ever had in my mouth. I can't help but think, where is Mom? She has such strong hands.

I stretch my arm to the locker, groping to find my phone. Dad moves into the room and tells me to lie down. Then he asks, "What do you need?"

"I want my phone to check on things," I say.

Dad says, "I'll tell you what's going on. What do you want to know?"

"How is Sergei?"

"He is fine. He's working on the plans for getting out of orbit and back on course for Earth."

"Already?"

"Already."

"What about the samples? Are they okay? I wasn't much help on the planet."

"That's fine. The samples are perfect. The second trip to the surface finished the mission as planned. You were mostly along for the ride anyway. We wanted to give you a little exposure to flying the shuttle, a chance to improve your piloting skills, and a taste of more gravity."

"I was terrible, Dad."

"You were great. I'm sure sending you out there for the

first time when you were coming down with a bug turned it into a special kind of struggle."

Jordan comes into the room with his equipment bag. "I'm going to check your throat and fever again," he says and pulls out a tongue depressor. "And now for the words every doctor longs to say: Open up and say, 'ah.'"

I let my mouth fall open and he peers in, pushing down on my tongue with a depressor. It chokes me a little.

"We'll start the adaptive antibiotics now. It means an injection of nanobots. I'll monitor the treatment and make sure your phone is synchronized with the Medibot so you can do that, too. Ted, will you check her phone and tell me what install she has of MediBot?"

Dad starts rummaging through my locker. "It's on the shelf, Dad," I tell him. He pulls it out, lights it up, and swipes through a few screens.

"Here it is," my dad says. "We included it in the system image I used for her. Install 67.2."

"Good. That's the right one. I hate reloading that. Okay, make sure it's running and I'll oobi with the ship and sync everything."

The two of them talking creates a low hum of deep voices that I don't even try to decipher until I hear Jordan say my name. "Okay, Rose Marie. It's time for the shot."

It is a tiny needle in my upper arm. A sting. My arm feels bruised right away.

"What is wrong with me?" I ask. I have never felt this awful in my life.

Jordan answers, "You have an infection. We think there's bacterial build-up in some of the kitchen equipment or in the suit you wore to the planet. We're looking into it now. What you have to concentrate on, is getting better. I have learned that getting sick never comes at a convenient time."

Jordan leans against the bunk like he's got nothing else to do than keep me company.

"Here, let me tell you a story to illustrate," Jordan continues. "When I was a kid, like ten years old, I had a big project due for school. It was probably a diorama of 9-11 or the signing of the Declaration of Independence or something. But I had not finished it in time. Not at all. It was fall quarter right before winter break. The afternoon before it was due, I was wandering around the front yard alone. We had a hill that had one hump and then went sliding straight into the street. Our grass was terrible because of all the trees. Very sparse. Lots of moss. Anyway, I had the bright idea of eating some of the dirt and moss in order to make myself sick. You know what happened, Rose Marie?"

"What?"

"Nothing. Nada. I did not get sick at all. I very much needed to be sick, but I had to go to school and face the teacher with my sorry lack of homework."

I am starting to get tired again, but I like hearing this story. "What did it taste like?"

"Being sick? Oh! You mean the dirt and moss? I don't remember what the dirt and moss tasted like. But moss is yellow-green in color and spongy and furry in texture. That made it quite unappetizing. Ugh. And here's something sort of funny that happened later that year. Maybe a year later. One morning, I pulled out the bottle of red fruit punch my mom always had in the fridge and gulped down about half of it. It was always this large glass bottle with a skinny mouth because she didn't like to store food or drink in plastics. My mom was so paranoid about plastics. Anyway, my stomach was sloshing with half a bottle of red fruit punch and breakfast, and I don't know what all, and I walked out the door to the bus stop, down the path by the bushes in front of the house, then you know what? I threw up right into the azaleas. You know what happened then, Rose Marie?"

"What?" I say and smile.

"I got to stay home from school. Apparently, that is how

you get out of school. You chug a half-gallon of fruit punch and toss your cookies right into the azaleas. No eating dirt or moss necessary. Tossing your cookies always gets you out of school."

I try to smile. I try to ask what an azalea is. I try to point out that he wasn't really sick in either story. But I am really tired and drowsy and I think he can figure that out by himself. Jordan starts to talk to my dad and their voices become a buzz again, which vibrates into a lullaby that my mom used to sing.

Chapter 29

I don't know if it was because I was sick, but the sensation on the surface of Finch-Hernandez can be summed up in one word: down. When you're on a ship that has only about a quarter g, down and up are stronger than right and left (or starboard and port), but it's not a huge difference. Standing on the planet, my whole self being pulled on at once toward the ground—that is when the word "down" takes on more meaning. I felt tied to the ground. "Up" felt like it floated above us.

Maybe I should say being on the planet also felt like the word "heavy." I became a heavy body in addition to my usual size.

So now I have a better idea of down and heavy and weight. But I also have a better idea of hollow. The ship feels kind of hollow without my mom. My head has cleared and I wonder why I'm alive.

I would trade with her, you know. Give my life for my mom's and all that. She should be the one on this ship—not me, the extraneous, accidental passenger.

We haven't changed the bunk assignments at all, but

our room seems very different. My dad sleeps in Mom's bunk every night. He took one of her jumpsuits, wrapped it up, and buried it in his locker like a treasure. "It's funny," he says. "We were living exactly the life we wanted. When you happened, we became a complete family. The work. The ship. All of it was going just how we wanted—even the stuff we didn't plan. And we were only halfway through. You think you have forever, but you don't."

Chapter 30

I'm getting a check-up from Jordan. He wants to make sure I am fully recovered. I don't know what he or I would do differently if I weren't fully recovered, but I'm not going to question this. Jordan tells me to keep drinking lots of fluids and sleep when I am scheduled to sleep. Sure.

At the end of the examination, he says, "Would you help me for a while in the farm? Come on. It'll be fun."

I get down from the exam bed and straighten my clothes. The farm is right next to the medical area. I can't say I've worked in the farm a lot. Sometimes, I've helped with harvests. And I had to learn all the procedures we had in place. But Jordan and Panchi do most of the day-to-day work.

Jordan hits the button to start the stereo in here. "They like softer music. I go with Miles Davis a lot." The sound of pianos and soft horns comes from the speakers.

"Here we are," he says when we get to the potatoes.

He lifts the lid for the potatoes. It has holes in it. Above, you find the foliage; below you find roots and water.

"Are they ready?" I ask.

"Yep. I think so," says Jordan.

"Can we pick some for dinner?"

"Let me check the schedule." Jordan pulls out his phone again and scrolls through the screens with his thumb. "Yeah, I can do that. Let me adjust the plan. Hang on."

Jordan starts tapping numbers into his meal plan organizer for the crew.

"Can I pick some potatoes while you're doing that?" I ask. "I think we could have a nice potato-based meal."

I like how moist the air is in the farm. I like the long rows of leaves. I like the different color lights for the plants that make for a long, low, multi-colored ceiling.

"Get some greens too," Jordan says. "I think we've got enough lettuce ready."

We work for a couple of hours, selecting potatoes and lettuce for dinner. The potatoes are nestled in their wet, brown roots below the separating lid. The lettuce grows in bunches above their lids. We take them to the galley and put them aside for now.

He fills two water containers for us. "Let's watch the plants grow for a little while," he says. I follow him back to the farm. He hands me the water containers and pulls out two folding chairs. They are made with a wide cloth with red stripes, that forms a hammock for your body.

"There," he says and he sits. I hand him a water container and drop into the other chair. "Okay, Rose Marie, how about some John Coltrane. I like that."

We sit for at least an hour listening to the songs, watching the plants, and smelling the wet farm air. I think about asking him what azaleas are—you know, from his story about throwing up after drinking fruit punch. But I could look that up, too. So I just lean back.

Eventually, he has to go make dinner. It's his turn tonight. I stay behind for another dose of music and I want to switch to something new. Ethan Junior pointed me to some new bands yesterday and this is a good time to try them out. I hope it doesn't bother the plants, but I need a dose of something harder and a little mean. Call me moody. I don't care.

Chapter 31

Do you know what doesn't happen out here? You don't say goodbye much, if ever, because no one ever gets all that far away. I don't even say goodbye to Ethan Junior. We stop and start the endless message/voice/vid thread that is our friendship, without any formalities. Now, my mother has left the whole universe and I never got to say goodbye to her. She didn't even wake me up for the shuttle flight. It's like someone blasted a hole in the ship that is my life, brain, and heart. I am leaking air, thoughts, and feelings. Nothing is going to close that wound up.

Dad says I should talk to Abuela on a vid chat. I have been dodging that. I love my grandmother, but I'm not sure I can deal with her. She is not a difficult person or anything. But she is emotional and sensitive, and I know she is going to be thinking of Mom as her baby. What am I in that equation?

I should take a deep breath and talk to her. It's just going to get harder. Deep breath. Deep breath. Okay.

I send Abuela a message.

Hello Abuela

She must be on her phone, she answers so fast.

My little granddaughter! How are you?

I come right to the point.

Do you want to set up a vid call?

Her answer surprises me.

Darling. I love you. Let's talk in a week or so.

I didn't expect her to want to wait. Maybe we are more alike in our grief than I thought. I try again.

Abuela?

She responds:

Honey, I just can't talk right now. I love you so much! So much!

I can only answer one way now.

I love you too

I think I still don't know how to deal with her right now. Maybe it's good we're light years away from each other. It is easier and harder this way. Easier because I don't have to go to the effort of dealing with her grief. Harder because there doesn't seem to be anyone I can talk to.

Chapter 32

One of the best windows to leave orbit around Finch-Hernandez is coming up in twelve hours. I am helping Sergei with the flight plans for the rest of the trip. And those plans are mostly done, but the WSC wants to prep me and Sergei and have Dad take on some of the navigation oversight. Why train me? I think it's part of my education, and—if you haven't caught on—also the others are already overworked trying to fill in for my mom and Jackie. (I say that like the two of them are taking a day off or something.) I am required to help out, but it's work I want to do and I am halfway trained to do it. My mom made sure of that.

I have a strange mental loop going on. I'm dying to tell Mom about everything that I'm doing because she's gone, but she's gone and I can't. Sometimes I wake up and I've totally forgotten about what happened to her. Those are the best moments. Then they are followed by the worst moments.

Sometimes I dream about her. She's mostly a feeling in my dreams, like she's in the same room with me. I hope I have those dreams forever.

In the workroom, I heard Jordan ask if we could stay at Finch-Hernandez to recover from everything—the next acceptable window of time to leave would be in three Earth months. The captain shot down that idea really quickly. "Delay is not on our side," he said. "We do not have all the time in the world."

When we left orbit from Kepler-917 and from Kepler-804, it was like a party. When we made those departures, we had done what we needed to do and had worked out all the problems as they came up. This time, it feels like a forced march. Everyone seems tightly wound and ready to lose their temper, but also determined not to.

Chapter 33

Sergei asked me to stay on the flight deck for the whole process of leaving orbit. He said he isn't used to being in charge of it. I think he also wants me to keep him company.

"This won't take long," he says as I sit in one of the pilot seats. "Some things require two people. You are best for this. Mel and Jack trained you."

"Sure," I say in a wary voice. "What do you want me to do first?"

"Make sure nothing falls apart while I maneuver us. We need to face Earth and get up to FTL speed. I'll take care of that."

"Okay," I answer. I start to check through everything to make sure Sergei has done the setup right. This is the correct procedure. It's not me second-guessing him. Between you and me though, it's also a good way for me to get oriented and find my way as a co-pilot.

As I verbally list each item I check, he confirms each item. This is working fine.

"WSC has sent corrected coordinates," he says when we're done with my list of items. "Let's make their adjustments now."

Translation: he'll show me what he does as he makes the adjustments and I'll watch. There are a lot of coordinates to check and double-check. He keys in the changes, then I check them, then he checks them again. (We really have to get this exactly right.) Once that's done, Sergei starts to look more relaxed.

He hits the com on his phone and says, "About to leave orbit of Finch-Hernandez now. Join us!" Then he leans back and says to me, "Are you ready?"

"I'm ready," I answer.

Jordan arrives first. "Panchi and John-Michael are in the sample storage area working on the new material. They're not coming out for this."

Then my dad and the captain arrive. We all face toward the front of the ship. Sergei and I go through the launch procedure until we get to the last part, where you push the two buttons that starts the shift into FTL flight.

"Okay, you hit it, Rosie," Sergei orders. "You have to push them at the same time."

"Now? Yeah?" I say.

"Yeah!" he says.

I press the buttons and the engines start ramping up. FTL drive is engaged. The ship is humming again.

We are going "home."

Chapter 34

The captain has ordered us to have a meal together for John-Michael's birthday, August 14. He said, "I know it doesn't feel the same, but we should do this."

I think most of us would rather pretend there are no birthdays anymore on the ship. Well, I would have.

Right after the announcement, Jordan asked to let him help plan it. Panchi agreed and said the two of them would do it together. John-Michael looked sheepish, pushed his shoulders together, and said, "That is so much attention."

I didn't want to help or be involved or anything. I wanted to stay in my little lagoon of work with Dad and Sergei.

But here it is, hour 1800, and I am pulling myself to the galley area. When I get there, I am a little stunned at how much food is on the table. I think everyone has an extra serving, maybe two extra servings. I feel a little sick at the idea of the dessert—a double packet of fruit gel.

The fruit gels were a special thing between my mom and me. I don't want other people to have it. I don't want it either.

Panchi is scrolling through her phone. She taps open

the com. "John-Michael, we're ready for you."

"Yes, my love," he responds.

Jordan, already there with Panchi, greets me. "Come through, Rosie."

"Why is there so much food, Jordan?" I ask.

"Rosie," he says and reaches for my hand. "Rosie, you know how we had to redo all the portioning of food to cover feeding nine people instead of eight? Right?"

All of a sudden, the ship feels like it's spinning. My head is full of a rushing sound. I shouldn't have even had to ask. I know we were rationing food because of me. I know it was stretched. That was how food worked on the Grimm Explorer. Being hungry is a celebration of life, we said.

Now I think—I know—being full is something that I will associate with grief. When there are fewer people, there is more food. I don't want any of it.

I can't stand it. There's no escape. So I take myself out of there, rush through the other quarters and the burned-out section, and stuff myself into my bunk, blanket over my head. There is no way off this stupid ship. It's a trap, a cage, a zoo. It puts us all on display to each other. I want to hide.

And here I am hiding.

Dad comes in and pulls up next to my bunk. "Honey," he starts, but he doesn't continue. He reaches out for my hand and takes it in the kind of handshake Mom used to make with me. And I lose control.

My chest is crushed, and I'm heaving with every breath. My face is hot and full of tears and snot as they come out of my eyes and nose. Dad keeps holding my hand.

Then he leaves for a minute and comes back with a damp cloth. He wipes my face with it as I rotate toward him. My forehead is smoothed with the cloth. My skin wiped clean. I still feel hot in the face.

"Oh, Rose Marie," he says. "I love you very much, and I'm proud of you and so glad to have you as my family.

Right now I am trying to get through the days just like you are. But you should know I think one of my main jobs is to give you as much of a childhood as I can. I might not be very good at it, but I'm going to try." He pauses, rubs his cheek, then continues. "Part of that means I'm your parent and I have to make sure you can be a functioning member of society. We're going to try to join them, okay? Respecting and celebrating others is an important skill. It's not always about you. Do you understand?"

"Yes. I think I'll come with you," I tell him. "Give me a minute. I want to wash my face."

"Good," he says. "That's for the best. Sometimes you play a role in someone else's life."

I heft myself out of the bunk and we go back through the different sets of quarters. I stop at the sink and Dad waits for me to wash up.

When we walk into the galley, everyone else falls silent. Then John-Michael raises his drink container and says, "Here's to you all. Thank you for the birthday dinner."

Then he hunches his shoulders a little and adds, "Who wants to hear about the time I crashed my bike into the neighbor's mailbox?"

"Oh, John-Michael! You were such a wild kid," says Panchi.

"I was an all-over-the-place kid. And that was a great bike. I had just gotten it for my birthday. It was orange and I had hauled it up to the top of the driveway—which was very steep—and went down as fast as I could. Daredevil fast. But I did not turn hard enough at the end of the driveway. Bang! Right into old man Johnson's mailbox. That was the first time I got stitches."

"Oh, John-Michael!" says Panchi again, smiling into his face.

I slip into my spot at the table and Dad sits next to me. We start around the table with the stories. I stay quiet, but the stories are all good, even the ones I've heard before.

They're the most comfortable ones.

My dad tells about how he learned to ride a bike by using his older sister's yellow bike. (The color of the bike always seems to be an important part of these stories.) His parents lived in an apartment that year because they were moving from Columbus, Ohio, to San Jose, California (right on the coast), and they wanted to rent before buying a house. The three kids and parents all lived in a two-bedroom apartment on the second floor. The apartment opened up onto an outside breezeway (he called it). He would go to the ground level and coast down the sidewalk from the breezeway into the parking space right in front of that. Over and over and over. He did this until he got the hang of balancing on the bike and then he pedaled away, into the parking lot. No mailboxes. No stitches.

"Your parents didn't try to teach you?" asks Jordan.

"Yes, they did," answers Dad. "My mom tried a few times to take me to the park and teach me, but we fought every time. She was very pushy. But I was an even more pushy kid and I wanted to do it myself. So she stopped trying. And I did it myself."

"That's how it goes with parents, sometimes," answers Jordan.

I'm not sure if anyone understands my life, but I love to hear about other people's lives. It adds to my own somehow. Gives me a little more context.

Chapter 35

It used to be my days seemed like they were made out of exercising and school assignments, punctuated with message, images, and vids shared with Ethan Junior or Abuela. Now I have more focused work in addition to school assignments and I struggle to exercise enough. Dad lets me slide more than Mom ever did.

I'm using my phone to track the workouts now, because I need to get them done. I carry around weights or wear a weight vest sometimes, too. Being on a planet really brought home to me how extreme it will be on Earth. Also, exercising makes me take a break from other things, like thinking. Or remembering.

Ethan Junior helps distract me, too. I force myself to message him when I wake up, so that I'm thinking of someone other than myself. He never leaves me hanging for too long.

Today, I say the same thing I say most days:

Morning, Earthling

He answers a half hour later:

morning space person

I'm back in the sample storage area when his message arrives, and send one right back to him.

Do you want to see the samples?

He replies:

sure

I take a picture of the now-full wall of samples just as Dad comes in. The picture shows the light brown to dark grey to rust-colored bins of sand and rocks with the blurred figure of my dad moving his right arm to grab onto the side of the room. Good enough. I send it to Ethan Junior.

"You're sending that to Ethan Junior?" he asks.

"Yeah," I answer, still looking at my phone.

Ethan Junior replies to my image with something totally unrelated.

why didn't you tell me about the book

I write:

What book?

His answer is surprising to me.

the one with all ur images
i thought it was something official you didnt tell me about
i am trying to decide if i should be mad at u

I have no idea what he's talking about. So I write back:

Again. What book?

Ethan Junior explains a little more.

theres some new book coming out that says its all
unauthorized images from u

I repeat myself, but now I'm the one feeling kind of angry. Very, very hot.

What?

He answers:

i take it u dont know. give me a sec. i'll show you.

The Ethan Junior feed gets quiet for while. I send him my thoughts without waiting—preemptive guessing?

i think it's from the hack.
And oh, I'm going to have to tell my dad about
this.

I don't think I did anything else wrong.
I can't remember opening any other weird messages.
Ethan Junior is back on the feed.
heres something from a store.
I hit it and there is the book. A big-looking, real-paper book. The cover is a shot you can tell is from the flight deck looking out to the stars, because it's framed with some of the interior of the ship. That's such a standard shot. (Am I really critiquing my own images here?)
I'm going to find my dad. Thanks for the info. Hope it's
nothing new. Really thanks. Back soon!
Dad has already left this part of the ship, so I jump forward, after him. He's all the way on the flight deck talking with the captain.
"Dad," I say.
"In a minute, honey, okay?" he responds distractedly.
"Um, can you come find me? It's important." I reply and leave.
I head for my bunk, not knowing what else to do with myself while I wait. I start looking around—which I really haven't done a lot of lately. I've been spending way more time on work for the ship, trying to help the rest of the crew. No time for feeds and lines and channels.
There is, in fact, a lot of talk about the book and I find it pretty fast. Several channels are selling it as a digital or hard copy product. My name is on there. But since I've never heard of this, I don't know how they can get away with that. Or how they got the images to begin with. The images supposedly go all the way from my first little kid shots through the landing at Finch-Hernandez—which was after the hack and my getting a new device with a new system image—which means my current device is compromised.
And I don't know what images I've taken in all that time. Or rather—I do know what images I've taken and they aren't all images I'd want posted anywhere or printed in a book for everyone to see.

There's a free preview of the book and I click through to it.

There are my five-year-old feet in big space boots. A tilted image of my fractured arm clearly taken with my other hand. There's my mom and Jackie drinking coffee together. (Oh, Mom, I miss you.) There's Mom and Dad sitting next to each other, arms aligned and touching. (Oh, Mom.) And Jordan pretends to sleep while floating that time we shut off the gravity magnet to make repairs. John-Michael and Panchi hold hands, Panchi looking off to the side and John-Michael looking at Panchi. The captain leans against the wall on the flight deck, back straight, arms crossed while Jackie stands behind him a little out of focus. There's even the image I sent to Ethan Junior of my bruised-up broken toe, looking green and brown and, yes, kind of gross. Oh, my mom's in the background of that too.

There are a few themed pages like one layout that has only images taken in the direction of Earth. But, other than those kinds of pages, the table of contents tells me that the book was arranged chronologically. And now I'm supposed to pay money if I want to see more. "See the intimate details," says the ad.

"What's going on, Rose Marie?" Dad arrives.

"All my pictures are for sale," I tell him.

"What do you mean?"

"All my pictures. All the ones I sent to Ethan Junior, like, ever. There's a book of them for sale. See." I show him the preview.

Dad takes my phone and uses his to contact the captain. "Andre?" he says into his phone. "Do you have time to talk?"

"What's going on?" The captain's voice comes back over the phone, which is on speaker.

"Rose Marie's new phone is compromised too. Can we get the crew together to talk about possible threats and a course of action?"

"Yes, Ted," the captain answers. "But I want you to

figure out a recommended course of action."

A group com to everyone comes through almost immediately.

We meet in an hour in work room 2 to discuss a   possible
breach of Rosie's phone.

I really hope I didn't do anything wrong. Maybe I'm just a victim of circumstance. Maybe I was too caught up in the things that were happening and all the new work for me. I guess I think I'm guilty because I thought the phone was always taking too long to process images when I sent them to Ethan Junior—but I never said anything.

I wonder if I can ask my dad to explain how there can be a book about me, by me, with my pictures, but I didn't have anything to do with creating it. I know any potential security breach is more important. But I worry this issue will get lost in the conversation if I don't say anything. Is it a selfish thing to ask about? I'm going to ask anyway. I'll try to wait till it's not an interruption, but I know I'm going to be selfish and ask.

Chapter 36

An hour later, we're all in work room 2. Everyone keeps to the perimeter, stuck to the walls almost.

The captain starts talking first. "Rosie's phone has a virus. When she sends an image or vid, that image or vid is duplicating to a second location on Earth. Ted? What else do we know?"

"Okay, I've located the background virus and discovered that it's been running on her device as well as the previous device she was using, when she was originally hacked. I looked through all the data on her phone and found nothing that would compromise the mission beyond the intellectual property of the people on the ship. That is partly true because most of Rosie's work up till recently has been school assignments or her own projects."

"There's little that could compromise the mission from her phone," Panchi interjects.

"Yep, that's what I'm saying," replies my dad.

"I use Mom's devices for a lot of that work," I add. "She had all the right tools."

"We need to be careful, though," says Sergei. "But

what about DMZ containment? Shipboard systems have DMZ that should contain this sort of thing?"

"The DMZ passed everything through from Rosie's phone. Also, I went through the functions of the virus and they were limited to sending files—yes, that's bad enough—but since it was Rosie's phone they were pretty much limited to her personal images and movies."

"Captain?" Panchi asks. "Have we received any requests or communications about this?"

"So far, no," the captain responds. "And we might not have the capacity to worry about this if there are no overt threats and no hacks that mean someone can remotely control the ship."

My dad starts talking again. "Rose Marie, did you use your phone for any of the work you're doing with Sergei and me? I know you just said, you're mostly using Mom's equipment, but tell us more about how you work."

"I keep work and personal stuff separate," I say. "It wasn't intentional. My phone has become something I use for messaging Ethan Junior. Also, for school and for the stop-motion movies I make and games and things. Mom had all the right software for the navigation and piloting. So since she—" I stop, feel a choke starting, swallow, then start again. "Since she has been gone, I've used her devices. Before then, I didn't really have much data besides school assignments, pictures, games, and vids. Nothing official anyway."

"Okay." My dad takes in a deep breath. "Okay."

The captain ends the meeting. "Ted, you run diagnostics on the ship's systems. And get Rosie another new device. Recycle the parts on this one. Rosie, set up new accounts for all your messaging again. Everyone, check for malware and viruses on your personal devices. We're going to have to keep moving now and don't have a lot of resources to stop and dwell on this."

That night, after I have been in bed for a while, Dad

comes into our quarters. I listen to him get out of his clothes. He's breathing heavily, rubbing his face a lot, but not making a lot of noise.

"Dad," I say.

"Oh, honey. You're up," he answers.

"I can't sleep," I say. Then I add, "Are you going to be okay?"

"I don't know. We've worked through everything. I can't seem to find any malicious activity happening on the ship's network. I don't know. This is really hard right now. I think I've done everything I should, but then I've missed something. This is bothering me—I should have known better." His voice softens. "Of all the things that happened, this is something I personally could have prevented. I tossed off the hack like it was nothing, like it was the same problem I've handled five hundred times before. I didn't even try to see that it was a new situation." He takes a deep breath. "Okay. I need to shake this off and keep working. But, wow, I messed up on this one."

"Is there anything else you can do, Dad?"

"Keep working, honey. Sometimes that's all you can do. And be honest with yourself. And don't hide the mistakes."

Chapter 37

We are officially out of reach of the Finch-Hernandez solar system and heading for Earth. I guess we've been heading back to Earth since all the way back at Kepler-917 because the trajectory has been a kind of lopsided circle. No more stops until the last one now, in a little less than a year.

On the flight deck with everyone, waiting for a WSC vid conference, I am full of impatience. I am full of many different kinds of impatience, in fact. I want this meeting to be over. To get back to my work. To get away from everyone. To watch a new vid Ethan Junior posted. To figure out what the deal is with that book of my pictures. To get to Earth. To walk around on Earth. To stop feeling weird and crushed about my mom. All different kinds of impatience.

I will always feel weird and crushed about my mom.

The main screen on deck flicks on. It's Ethan Junior's dad and a couple other people. The oldest, grayest person on the screen (a man) says, "Welcome!"

"Thank you," replies the captain.

"We wanted to meet with everyone at the start of this

last leg of the mission. You all should be congratulated again. And again!" says the old, gray man.

"Thank you," repeats the captain.

"I know this is a difficult time. And there's still a lot to do. We can send a shuttle out to you when you're about one week out. I want all of you to think about whether or not we should send the shuttle with supplies or some other kind of relief. We currently think it would only serve to introduce risk and cause delay. But we wanted to ask you all if there are any critical needs."

"Thank you," says the captain—again. He continues, "We will probably forgo the shuttle, but we'll want to do a better assessment first. I know of nothing right now that would necessitate the trip. On the other hand, something might happen between now and then. It's months away. When do you need a final answer?"

"We can have a final answer 30 days out."

"Okay. Done. We'll make a preliminary answer now— which is 'no shuttle'—but we'll make the final call later, one month out."

"Alright. Jorge?" The old gray man leans to his left. "Will you follow up with Heidi on the timing of that? Michelle, Ken, and Randeep will be involved as well. Loop Evan in on this too—she'll want to know about it so her team can coordinate."

I have been in exactly two of these meetings before. I know I am going to have as much trouble paying attention now as I have in the past.

Jorge sends me a personal message. It is a massive surprise to me to hear from anyone new.

> *For these meetings, we have the folks at WSC trained to say our names when they want to ask someone specific a question.*

I respond in my own elegant, articulate way.

> *What? Why?*

And he answers.

So we know when to pay attention. Yes?

And that is especially funny because next thing I know, they are saying my name.

"Rose Marie?" Jorge, the guy to the left of the old, gray man, is talking.

First, I am surprised (again) at the sound of my name. Then I answer. "Yes?"

"Make sure you let the team know if you have any requirements for the shuttle in case we send it. Give them to Ted."

"Oh, like what?" I answer. I have such a great way with words.

"Medical requests, equipment, things like that," says Jorge.

"Okay. I'll let him know." I am secretly thinking that Jorge was just trying to follow up on his direct message.

"Talk to Dr. Banks, too, about re-entry. Tell him that we'll have the standard equipment ready for everyone's reintroduction to full gravity, but we want to know how serious or different the situation is going to be for you."

Oh. I get it now. I'm going to be the special case because of growing up on the ship. They are probably going to want to learn a lot from what happens to me physically. And here I was, not really worrying about it. Ha. Now I am officially freaking out about it.

Chapter 38

I'm sending Ethan Junior a message after the meeting.

I was just in the strangest meeting.

He answers.

what happened

And I answer him trying to get across what that WSC meeting was like for me. I explain:

WSC planning meeting about getting back to Earth. They are all of a sudden concerned about me. I think THEY think I'm in all kinds of trouble physically.

Ethan Junior doesn't have much to say:

oh

Me:

Yeah. So I am feeling crazy right about now. Maybe I AM in all kinds of trouble physically.

Ethan Junior:

is it the kind of trouble that means ur deformed

Me:

Well maybe.

Ethan Junior:

u dont look deformed in vid chats

Me:

Maybe I'm not going to be able to move around by myself or something.

Ethan Junior:

how were u on that planet

Me:

It felt—I felt—very heavy. But I was also getting sick. So ... Yeah. I felt heavy.

Ethan Junior:

ill still be ur friend. dont care if ur deformed or not

Me:

That is just the sweetest thing.

Ethan Junior:

moment of seriousness. itll be weird to see you. looking forward to the weirdness.

Me:

My first days on Earth are going to be in a hospital. Can you visit?

Ethan Junior:

i will visit no matter what

And—all of a sudden—I am scared to be on Earth. Not because of the dreaded physical problems, but because of seeing Ethan Junior. I have no experience in this. It's almost a year till then and that is a long time, but it is only one year, not fifteen, or three. One year. Less.

Maybe I should work out even more or wear weights all the time instead of just sometimes so I won't be such a weak body when I'm there. Maybe I should pay more attention to the news. Maybe I should study fashions. Maybe I won't have time for any of this because of trying to step up as co-pilot and everything.

Chapter 39

My days since Finch-Hernandez are divided not only between exercising and working with Sergei to help him be the navigator and pilot of the ship, but also I have to carve out time to work with Ms. French, my school counselor, and a new special teacher, Dr. Ron Maney.

After my mom died, there was no one with enough time to take over as my on-board teacher and lead my home-based (or rather, ship-based) education. So the WSC, the Orlando, Florida school board, and my dad contacted Dr. Maney to work with me. Dr. Maney is a teacher at a local Orlando high school, Westshore Senior High. He's got a PhD in American History and he seems pretty cool. He is very pale with dark hair and has the roundest face ever. He has a dark moustache. I would say it's a rather thick moustache. You can't see his mouth when he talks. That's how long his moustache is. I probably pay too much attention to the moustache when we're on a vid chat.

He's in charge of making sure I do my assignments and reading and figuring out how to help me when I have a question or trouble with the material.

And yes, this is one of the things that ultimately makes my mom's death seem so final, the change of the school routine, the take-over by Dr. Maney, the need for me to be more involved in keeping track of everything. It hurts my throat and my body to think of her, I'm punched over and over, even though each of those punches hurt less and less. Yes, I've never been punched, but I've seen it on vids. Which is worse in real life, punching or the blows that land on a person after your mom dies? I think real punches are easier than what this grief feels like.

I've made my own routine; it looks very much like the old routine with Mom, but it's mine now. All that school stuff usually happens in the morning for a few hours and then I pick it up again at the end of the day and finish off any assignments that aren't done yet. Today's typical.

This morning I only have two things to do. First, I have to proofread the final paper for a special unit all Florida-based high schoolers have to take on intractive competency. This is just the usual intractive-awareness material. I just have to demonstrate I can deal with basic amounts of digital and social engineering. The second thing I have to do this morning is a math unit. Then I want to spend a little time running or spinning as well as some weights—always some work on the weights. One two three. Uno dos tres. Ahdeen dvah tree. Workouts in three languages, more or less.

I'm being light-hearted right now about the workouts, but, to be honest, they have really intensified, because I have intensified them. I get more worried as time goes on. Without Mom, I feel so much more on my own. I have just under a year to be ready for full Earth-level gravity. I've re-doubled my efforts on weights—which I hate. Instead of promising to do more, I am actually doing extra things and wearing the wrist weights daily. The cardio workouts are about the same, except I try to add weights on my limbs for those, too.

The rest of the time, I try to help Sergei. Yes, the ship

itself has autopilot programs that could get us eighty-five percent of the way back. But missing by fifteen percent would be pretty tragic. Someone on ship has to make the adjustments and monitor the progress. Actually, it should be two someones, like my mom and Jackie. But the way it is now, it's like one-and-a-half persons with Sergei and me. And sure, the WSC is looking over our shoulders too.

Sometimes I shadow him. Sometimes I'm doing something that would take him fifteen minutes, but takes me two hours. I am trying.

Working with Sergei seems so much more important than school. It is probably a good thing Dr. Maney has the job of keeping me from dropping out. He's like an extra oxygen unit on a space walk.

But it would be funny if I dropped out of high school to fly a spaceship.

Chapter 40

Today's plan includes homework, work for the mission, and exercise, but my real goal is to start making a new vid. I've got at least four hours of totally free time today and I am very much looking forward to doing something with stop motion again. It's been a while. I want to make something new for the channel. And I just want to kind of work through the actions in a story step by step.

So the first thing I do when I wake up is nothing. Well, not nothing. I continue lying in bed completing a mental list of what I need. Characters: two snakes, a crocodile, and an ibis. The set will be in the burned-out section of the ship. I want that charred look. The story will take place in Giza or Cairo—wherever the pyramids are. I'll look that up later.

I can superimpose the Egyptian background, but I want a base setting that won't look metallic and the color of one part of the wall in the burned room is perfect.

Now that I have a plan, it's time to make the parts and pieces. I get out of bed, then stop in the bathroom latrine area to clean up and brush my teeth. I have no need to change clothes so I head all the way back to the back of the project area, next to the sample room.

Here, I make the snakes, crocodile, and ibis. I use a few pieces of plastic that were soon-to-be-recycled—some of which I cut into small fragments to help shape the characters. I pause to fantasize about being allowed to print out some tiny bones to make the bird. Since that is not going to happen, I start using shape and shadowing to define her (the bird is a she). On Earth, she would have a dark head, white-colored body, and dark legs. On a spaceship she has shape and shadowing because I don't have a lot of materials for coloring the foil.

Once I've got the animals made, I head over to my "set."

Sergei is in the galley and he's got one of his tubes of food which he thinks of as treats. He has rationed them out for this whole mission. It's some kind of meat and veggie combo. Or maybe it's borscht. It's purple anyway.

"What do you have there, malyshka?" he asks.

"They're characters for my next stop-motion project. It'll be set in Egypt."

"Let me watch, yes?"

"Sure. It's a slow process, though. You've been warned."

It's nice to have someone to talk to while doing this. We probably look more like we're hanging out than anything else. Sergei's on his phone most of the time, which means I don't feel like he's hovering over me.

We chat while I go through the scene. The snakes and the crocodile argue about who the pyramid is a monument for. They go back and forth while the ibis watches them from a nearby perch. Soon, the snakes start biting at the crocodile who snaps back at the snakes. Next thing you know, all three are mortally wounded. Then the ibis flies down and says the pyramid is a tomb, she just didn't know it was going to be their tomb as well. Lesson learned too late for the snakes and crocodile.

"What's your favorite planet, Rosie?" Sergei asks me.

"You know, from our mission."

"I don't know, Sergei. By all rights, I should hate Finch-Hernandez, but I love it, too. The weird one-sided rotation. The fact that I got to walk on it. The pink and rust and red and brown colors. But it's where Mom and Jackie died. So I guess it's not that Finch-Hernandez is my favorite, but it is the one I think about the most." The ibis continues to look thoughtfully at the snake. "And to be honest, I don't have much of an emotional connection to Kepler-917 and Kepler-804. I literally used to call Kepler-917 'the noodle-colored planet' when talking to Ethan Junior."

"That makes sense," replies Sergei.

I return the question to Sergei. "What is your favorite planet?"

"Easy, it's Kepler-804," he answers. "Because of water and rocks. It was the first planet other than Earth that I got to walk on. It felt like walking around inside waterfall. Yes, I liked Kepler-804. It was fun, too. We laughed and joked. Jack and your mom were hilarious together. Great fun."

At one point, Sergei takes a break, returning with a tablet. "I nearly forgot about the call with my mom," he tells me.

"Can you do that here? I'd like the company."

"That's just what I planned."

Sergei sits on the ground, just out of frame of my story and starts a session. "Privyet! Kak dyela?"

They go back and forth in Russian, I think Sergei and his mom are just passing the time of day. She kind of fusses over him, that much I can tell from her tone of voice. And he kind of likes it.

After he shuts down the vid call, he looks at me, "I miss my mom sometimes."

"Me, too," I respond.

"Oh, Rosie—I did not mean anything."

"Neither did I. Sorry to be moody."

"I get it. You miss your mom."

"Yeah. I miss my mom."

Chapter 41

Today, when I join Sergei on the flight deck, he is really quiet. I log in and check my projects.

"What's going on?" I ask Sergei.

"Same stuff—different day. Closer to Earth. Still in space," he responds.

I look at his face. His already-pale face is looking so much more pale, like he's almost green. And he's sweating.

"Sergei? Are you feeling okay?" I ask more seriously.

"Not so good, Rosie."

"Do you want me to get Jordan up here?"

"I don't know. It will pass."

"I think I'm going to call Jordan."

I tap open the com and enter a message to Jordan:

I think Sergei is sick. Come to the flight deck?

He sends a message back right away:

Be right there.

It's about five minutes before Jordan gets up front, and Sergei has leaned back and closed his eyes. When Jordan puts his hand on Sergei's forehead, Sergei starts at the touch. But Jordan keeps his hand there, firm against his skin.

"It's just me, buddy," Jordan says. "Who'd you think it would be?"

"I don't know, I feel turned around," replies Sergei. "Glad it's you, friend."

"Okay. Let's not get too emotional about it. But I have to say you do feel like you have a fever. Let's try something more objective." Jordan presses the glass of his phone to Sergei's skin and checks it. "Congratulations, Sergei, you have a fever of thirty-nine-point-four. You need to get into your bunk and start drinking fluids."

"Rosie, start with tasks on your list. Let me know if anything weird happens," Sergei orders me, but weakly.

"I got it. I'll do my best. Should I send a message to WSC?" I answer.

"Yeah. Send it to Jorge Mahon. He will get you anything you need," says Sergei.

Jordan takes Sergei by the arm, gently, "If this is what Rose Marie had, I'll start the adaptive antibiotics. Are you going to be okay with nanobots?"

"I think I do not have a choice, Jordan. I feel awful. I ache all over. Even my neck hurts," states Sergei.

"You'll be okay, Rose Marie?" asks Jordan.

"Yeah, I'll be fine," I answer. "Sergei is the one who's sick."

Now that I am alone on the flight deck, I do not feel "fine." Sergei has what I had? How long would it take to transmit that? He should have been sick before. I don't even know what I had or where I picked it up. Something from one of the kitchen tubes?

I feel like there are a lot of things I should be doing, but I don't know where to start. So I start by getting in touch with someone else. That will be easier than going it alone. Right?

I send a message to Jorge Mahon.

TO: Jorge.Mahon@WSC.gov

138

REPLY-TO: Rose.Williamson2@WSC.gov
Mr. Mahon,
Sergei is sick and went to his bunk to rest. I don't
know how long he will not be able to work. I am
going through my assignments. Let me know if I
should do something else or contact someone else
about this.
Thanks,
Rose Marie Hernandez Williamson

I have to emphasize how much I hate my WSC addresses—old and new. How hard would it be to get all of my name in there, you know? I wouldn't mind *Rose.Marie.Hernandez.* *Williamson@WSC.gov* or *RoseMarie.HernandezWilliamson@* *WSC.gov*. You'd think they would have figured out how to deal with names like mine. I can't be the first person with multiple names who works there. Rose Williamson sounds like someone else—like my two aunts merged into one big, older lady. And the Hernandez? That is important to me. It should always be there because it's part of who I am. It includes my mother and my mother's family—translation, my family.

After about ten minutes with no response—the system is so passive and so slow—I start to go through my assignment list, picking out the things I can get done by myself.

After an hour and a half, Jorge Mahon responds.

TO: Rose.Williamson2@WSC.gov
REPLY-TO: Jorge.Mahon@WSC.gov
Rose Marie,
Keep doing what you're doing.
Tomorrow, let me know if Sergei is any better or
worse. I'll forward this status and tomorrow's status
up the chain of command and to anyone else who
should be aware of it. We'll let you know if you
should do anything differently.
Thanks,
Jorge

So that's out of the way. I wonder why it took him so long to respond. Maybe it's lunchtime or something. Or that's just how they work.

Jordan messages me from Sergei's quarters:

Rosie. Go check on Panchi. She's in back working. Said she felt bad.

I log out of the ship's system and head back through the ship. When I go through Sergei's quarters, Jordan looks toward me, but he keeps holding Sergei's hand.

"Any better?" I ask.

"No," he answers and then repeats himself. "No."

When I get to the project room, Panchi is looking at her device trying to work, but clearly struggling. She's got a greenish, sweaty look too.

"Jordan said you weren't feeling well?" I say.

"Oh," Panchi responds, head down. "That is right. I feel very ill. I can't seem to see straight." Then she looks at the top of the room, eyes unfocused.

"Okay, maybe you should get to your bunk. I'll get John-Michael to help. Okay? Where is John-Michael?" I ask her.

"He is in the sample room." Panchi looks straight at me and I see how red her eyes are and that her face is kind of puffy. She does not look well. Let me say that again. Not well.

"Got it. I'll get John-Michael to help," I tell her.

In the next room with the samples, John-Michael is also engrossed in his work, but he glances up as soon as I come in the room.

"Hi. Uh, I think we need to get Panchi to her bunk." I say.

"She's sick?" asks John-Michael.

"Oh, yeah, she looks really sick. And she messaged Jordan, so it probably is serious."

"Yeah. She wouldn't say anything unless it was really bad."

John-Michael and I move back to the project room, get

Panchi away from her work and into her bunk area. Once we're there, John-Michael starts getting Panchi out of her clothes and I go back to the flight deck.

That's two people sick. I hope it is easier for them than it was for me. Being sick was horrible.

Okay, let's be honest for a quick second. That isn't my first thought. It's my second, more charitable thought. My first thought actually is that I am dreading the increase in my chores, tasks, and duties for the week or so they will be out of commission. Increased duties will be not quite so horrible to live through as being sick, but this will be a harder week for me too, that's for sure.

Chapter 42

At dinner time, Dad and I are having our supper together, but it's just the two of us.

Since Mom died, Dad has seemed kind of fake. It's like he is just going through the motions of being my father. And that's okay. I'm not a little kid or anything. But it all feels forced. And I, of course, feel lonely and awkward.

When do I not feel awkward? That is really just my normal. I shouldn't even notice, should I? But it's my condition to notice the awkward like noticing the air I breathe, which I guess I could do if I wanted to—after all, I've got total access to the ship's stats on air quality like everyone else on board.

Finally, my dad talks. "John-Michael is sick."

I am surprised. "He's sick, too?"

"Yeah. After dinner, I'm going to go check on everyone. See if Jordan needs any help. Will you clean up?"

"Sure. Yeah," I say.

"Will you also clean the latrine and shower area? It's John-Michael's turn, but you know, he's out of it," he adds.

"Of course," I say. Can one mentally hold one's nose?

I always try when the subject of my cleaning the latrine comes up. "Is this what I had? I don't even really know where that came from."

"Jordan narrowed it down partially. It wasn't a bacterial problem with the space suits or anything in the kitchen. So we just don't know."

I question this. "We just don't know?"

"I should have said, we tested all the common areas, and those came up negative. We tested your suit and that came up negative. The process for cleaning the latrine and galley might have flushed it. So: we just don't know."

I feel like I want to push back, like the process of disagreeing with him and accusing him and Jordan of something (I don't know what) would be a pleasure. A line needs to be drawn. I think. Maybe.

Now I think I am going to spend the rest of the mealtime trying to think of things to say and rejecting my ideas for things to say because they were too obvious or too insensitive.

We are done eating relatively quickly, having not talked about anything else but sickness and chores and not knowing where the sickness came from.

Dad heads down toward John-Michael's quarters and I clean up the galley, wiping food trays, putting utensils and everything in the dishwasher sterilizer, and starting it on the gentle cycle.

Then I'm onto cleaning the latrine and shower. More wiping. Some flushing. Some hosing. Nothing too terrible since everyone else is very good about their chores. Then again, maybe this is where the sickness came from. I repeat the whole procedure. Clean. Wipe. Hose. Flush the lines. After all that work, I stop mentally holding my nose and go looking for my dad.

John-Michael and Panchi are both sleeping. Panchi looks so small in her bunk, turned away. The blanket drapes her body. She has a really tiny waist and the blanket outlines the swoop of her hips. Her husband faces outward, face slack, arms bent, hands together like they're mid-clap, or like he's praying while he's sleeping.

In Sergei and the captain's quarters, I find Dad, Sergei, the captain, and Jordan. Sergei's in bed and Dad and the captain are arguing with Jordan. I hover near the doorway. It looks like Jordan is sick too, and Dad and the captain are trying to get him to lie down and take it easy.

"I have to watch Sergei and the other two," Jordan insists. "And start checking the farm for contaminants."

"Show Ted what to do; he can take over," orders the captain. "At least on monitoring the sick."

"Show me, too," I interrupt.

Their heads all shift around together to look down at me.

"Okay, all of you. Okay," concedes Jordan. "God, I feel terrible. Open your MediBots. I'll sync them up—that's for both of you," he adds when he sees that I'm not following along even though I've just insisted on helping with this.

"Oh, oh. Sure," I say as I pull out my phone and tap through to MediBot.

"I've got Sergei on nanobots armed with adaptive antibiotics. I'm going to want the same for Panchi, John-Michael, and me. Which one of you wants to do the honors?"

"I'll do it," I suggest.

"And—no. I was going to elect Ted. Ted? You're good with that? Because I'm going down fast," Jordan says. "I really need to go lie down."

I thought he was taking volunteers. It must have been just a way of asking Dad to step in.

"I've got you," says my dad.

"Okay, I'm going to bed now. Take Rosie, I guess, I think," Jordan says. He starts holding onto the bunk. Then he moves to the doorway, followed by my dad. "Ted, thanks."

"You're going to be fine. Let me help you get settled now,

then I'll see to the others," Dad says.

It crosses my mind that Jordan is lucky because he has my dad there to comfort him. I realize that I'm very glad to have my dad here, too. I'm glad for his voice, for him trying to be a dad, even if it's forced. I'm just glad for him. And I miss Mom.

The captain takes a look at me and adds, "Come see me when you're done, Rosie. I want to figure out if we can rely on the ship's system and the WSC instructions—and you— while Sergei is sick."

Chapter 43

I watch as Dad injects the nanobots into Panchi and then John-Michael. I get them fresh water containers and damp cloths. John-Michael puts his hand up to the side of Panchi's bunk and she rolls toward it and holds on. They cannot see each other, but I see them from the side and both of them relax a little when they touch. Panchi has a small smile.

"You two okay for now?" my dad asks.

"Yes. We're okay," Panchi answers.

"I'm kind of itchy," adds John-Michael.

"I love you itchy or not," Panchi tells him.

"And I you, my sweet," says John-Michael. He is smiling, now, too.

"Uh, okay, I'll come check on you later," says Dad as his eyebrows cross and move up his face.

"Dad, the captain asked me to talk to him about what we need to do now that Sergei is sick." I'm halfway out of the room already.

"Okay, honey," he answers.

I hear Panchi say to John-Michael, "Did you ever change

your mind about wanting a little kid of our own?"

"I just wanted to be with you," answers John-Michael.

"And I with you, my love. And I with you."

Chapter 44

I find the captain on the flight deck. He looks at me with those dark round eyes that kind of protrude a little all the time. I never know what he's thinking.

He asks me to sit.

He starts the conversation. I expect a bunch of orders. "I've traded messages with the WSC. I want you to follow along with their instructions, but between the ship's systems and WSC's navigation, there isn't a lot to do right now as far as piloting goes. It's never a good time for illness, but I think it won't be much of a problem at this particular time."

"I'll go through my messages, okay? And then I have to go workout, yes?" I ask, feeling tentative.

"That's good. Have a good night." He dismisses me.

I stop at our quarters and swipe through all my feeds, responding to the very few messages that need to be acknowledged.

When I'm done with that, I head back to the exercise module. I start with large muscle groups and move to smaller ones: leg presses to arm exercises to working on my abs. After a certain number of these (forty, to be exact), it gets kind of meditative. One set of numbers leads to another set of numbers. I look forward to each new set as a different thing—though I have done this routine too many times for me to want to count them—yes, that many times. It's like each exercise has its own personality no matter the routine, but new and old routines all have the same spirit. And the numbers always take over. In English or Spanish or both. And yes, sometimes Russian, too.

I wipe myself and the equipment down and start to go back to our quarters. I can hear my dad and the captain talking in the galley. They are drinking from containers— probably with coffee in them.

My dad doesn't talk to me like an adult, so I don't really know what's going on with him. I know it's wrong, but I lurk and listen in.

"Thanks for everything today, Ted," the captain says.

Dad answers, "I need the work, Andre. I need to think about something else most of the time. Otherwise, I'm thinking about Melissa and that is still too hard."

The captain says something more personal than I have ever heard from him before. "Nighttime is the worst time. When it's quiet and there are no projects or meetings or communications to distract me, no crisis or sickness, no one is mad at anyone—it's at these hours when I look at her locker, her bunk. I pull out the ring she wore all the time. I trace along the smooth inside of it with my little finger. I wonder when she's going to come through the doorway." He pauses. "I'm getting through. Just another day. Just another second. Another minute. Another hour. We get closer to Earth, but I'm not sure quite what I'm waiting for—she won't be there, either. It feels like madness." He pauses again, a longer silence this time. "I didn't want to live my life alone. I wanted my life to be with Jack. I had found my life in her. And now she's gone. It feels so wrong."

"I can barely look at Panchi and John-Michael sometimes," adds my dad. He's on the same topic in a different way. "It hurts to see them so matched to each other. Even when they are both sick, they are in tune. Harmonized. So with themselves. You know, I hold one of Melissa's shirts at night. I'm ruining them with my scent. She's getting fainter."

I had never thought about the fact that both my dad and the captain lost their spouses. I think I'm sorry to be so wrapped up in my own loss. But I'm not sure if I am even able to think about other people the way I think about myself sometimes. Is it enough to acknowledge what others are going through when you can't help with anything or talk to them about it? I'm not sure if that acknowledgement (made only to myself) is to make me feel better about who I am or not. Is it a positive thing to be honest about when I'm not a good person? Or should I pretend to myself that I am always empathic and caring so it becomes a habit? I mean if I value something—like charity or niceness—shouldn't I try to act how I think a good person should act, even in my head?

I don't think I have the self-control to fake myself out like that.

Most of the time I feel like I can't make anything better. Everything seems to happen as it would anyway. Maybe I should just pay attention to what's in front of me. What I'm learning. What my chores and jobs are.

Let the universe be the universe.

And so I let the two mental universes who are my dad and the captain finish their conversion without me leaning on the wall outside the galley.

Chapter 45

When I finally get back to our quarters, I find my dad in his bunk reading through Jordan's resources, and checking the nanobot readout on Medibot for our sick crew members.

"Panchi is not getting any better," he reports. "John-Michael is about the same. Jordan looks like his case isn't as bad as the others."

"And Sergei?" I ask.

"He was the first case—after you, that is—and it looks like he's responding to treatment pretty well. They all have rashes and shortness of breath. Panchi is really having trouble. Sergei's symptoms have really eased up. He had Jordan to take care of him, though. I feel so overwhelmed with this work."

"Dad, you're doing great," I tell him, trying to be encouraging. I am not sure if it's working.

"I don't know honey. I worry. You know, I'm not perfect," he says and he smiles a little.

"Yeah, I know." I smile back. It's good to hear one of his self-deprecating jokes again.

"All right, thanks for the vote of confidence," he says continuing the tease. He pulls himself upright.

Then the captain comes into our quarters, pausing at the doorway. "Ted," he starts.

"Yes, Andre?" Dad responds.

"What have you found?" says the captain.

"I'm looking around for more background on the nanobots," Dad tells him. "Jordan has a lot of stuff compiled about living so long in quarter-g conditions. I'm trying to see if I should be worried about that right now and if it will influence the treatment."

"He was telling me that Yale published several studies on the circulation issues and increased risk of stroke with long-term living in low gravity," says the captain and he goes over to sit next to Dad.

Dad answers him, "Yeah! One of them had something on the decreased effectiveness of nanobots in low g—they depend on or are helped by full gravity when getting around the body in the bloodstream. Once again, optimally used on Earth, of course."

And with that, I leave the room. I can check on Jordan, Sergei, Panchi, and John-Michael in a non-medical way.

In Sergei, Panchi, and John-Michael's quarters, Sergei is the only one awake.

"Hey, you, malyshka," he calls out.

"You're awake," I point out.

"Yes, and I need something to look at. I've got earbuds. Tell me again. What's your channel with Ethan Junior?"

I take a deep breath. I used to cringe at the idea of people on board seeing my vids. Well, I used to hate people watching me work, too. Now, I know Sergei and Jordan saw many of the parts and pieces that that went into them while they were being made. Of course, these vids are the finished products. I hope Sergei will like them. I sort of know anyone on board who sees them will want the vids to be good. If it's even remotely possible to say they are great, my shipmates will say the vids are great.

"Look for 'Hurricanes and Rocks.' You'll know it's us if it says it's run by El Gato and La Gata. I hope you enjoy them."

"I will like them. I have seen very many creatures and scenes you made for your vids. Cute."

"Yeah—I think you've seen almost all the characters."

John-Michael and Panchi have slept through our whole conversation. I think I should leave them alone. Sergei already has Hurricanes and Rocks up and the top post is playing featuring an Ethan Junior rant about the weather in Florida. Sergei's eyes are closed though. I'm not sure if he's actually listening or just wants a distraction like white noise.

Oh, and there goes Ethan Junior! Shirt off, his scrawny, 15-year-old chest exposed. So pale. Ouch.

I go into the captain and Jordan's quarters. Jordan's asleep. I want them all to feel better, for their sakes, and not just so I have fewer chores.

Chapter 46

It is the next morning. I look over the side of my bunk and see Dad, in Mom's bunk again, arm flopped over the side. I do not remember him coming into our room last night. I was tired. He must be really exhausted.

I feel full of energy. Ready to bounce all day. I know that if I think of everything I have to do, it'll seem like too much. And sometimes that will mean I don't want to do anything at all. So I try to think of the one thing I want to do first. Today, that's food. I'm starving. I want, like, a big meal.

I unstrap my harness and slide out of bed. I keep very quiet (of course) as I move through the captain and Jordan's quarters. The captain is already up and gone. Jordan seems sound asleep.

Since the fire, the charred hallway that used to be Panchi and John-Michael's place has a different odor than the rest of the ship. If I had to move around the ship with only my sense of smell, this part of the ship would definitely be a kind of a landmark.

Panchi, John-Michael, and Sergei are all bunked out. Panchi looks somehow wrong in her bed. Her face is flat, her eyes open. Panchi looks gone. I think she's passed away. I start to yell, "Dad! Dad! Oh! Come here, Dad!"

Sergei, now wide awake, undoes his harness and moves out of his bunk.

I remember to hit the alarm on my phone, but the captain is coming in from the direction of the front of the ship and Dad is coming from the back of the ship.

John-Michael—looking even paler than ever, greenish, freckles stark on his face, red hair plastered with sweat to his head—is hitting at his straps, trying to get out of his bunk. He gets still and says in a quiet, serious voice, "Where is Panchi?" He's a gentle person. I have never heard him sound so wary and ready to be angry.

Dad is by the side of the bunks with Sergei, but checking Panchi's body. "She's right here in bed," he says. He looks to the captain, eyes wide.

The captain knows Panchi has passed, too. Dad continues to work. His phone has the healthcare provider version of Medibot running Panchi's vitals.

"There was no alarm, was there?" the captain asks.

My dad has his one hand around her wrist, the other on her forehead. His body is shaking. And then, he moves his hand over Panchi's face, closing her eyes. "Alarm? No. I didn't get one. It might have been set up so alarms just go to Jordan's phone, which he would have missed."

Dad inhales and bends to John-Michael's bunk. "John-Michael," he says. "Panchi is gone now. She's passed on."

John-Michael lets out a wail, a howl. The sound is so loud and fills the space. But I'm not going to cover my ears. I'm going to listen to every bit of it.

My dad moves away to clean his hands. The captain goes over to John-Michael, but he doesn't say anything.

Sergei tells me to go let Jordan know what's happened. "Go over there in person. Don't message or com it to him."

As I leave their quarters, the area is silent except for the hum of the ship's air vents and gravity generator. John-

Michael is turned away from everyone. Panchi's body does not look like a real body. It was the same with my mom and Jackie.

Chapter 47

Sergei is up and talking with the captain on the flight deck. Jordan (who looks like a wreck, but at least he's moving around) is with Dad in sick bay with Panchi's body. They are preparing it to be locked in cold storage in the shuttle bay with Mom and Jackie.

I am connected up with Ethan Junior. He's letting me rant and be upset. This conversation looks like a lot of his messages kind of mirror mine—repeating my worries but turning them around.

I say things like:

> *I feel like I started it all. I'm not sure what I did wrong. Do you think I passed it on to them?*

And he says things like:

> *you didnt start it. you just got it first. you didnt do anything wrong. didn't happen fast enough to have been caught from you.*

But then we're interrupted when I get a message from Dad, to check on John-Michael.

I send a quick *later* to Ethan Junior and move into John-Michael's area. His breathing is labored and his face is closed up in sleep and, I think, grief.

I message back to Dad.

Do you want me to wake him?

Dad sends back this message.

No, Medibot said his fever spiked. If he's not awake, don't wake him. Get a water container and put it with him so he can find it when he wakes up, tho.

Check on him in an hour too pls.

I do as I'm told. I get a fresh water container and put it in the bunk with John-Michael so he can't miss it when he wakes up.

Dad sends another message:

Pull the bedding from Panchi's bunk and get it to the sterilizer.

I wonder if I've got extra immunity from getting and surviving the sickness (if it is the same sickness). I pull Panchi's blanket. I take off the sheet. I bundle them up and take them to the clothes sterilizer and stuff them in, hitting the button to start the cleaning cycle.

If I do have extra immunity, I should take care of John-Michael and the others more—though it seems like Sergei and Jordan are already getting better.

I go back to John-Michael's bunk and see that he's awake now.

"Rosie," he says. "Would you get my phone? It's in my locker. I want to hear some music, please."

I take his phone out. "What do you want to hear?"

"Go to my playlists and start the one called 'Panchi'."

I spin through his lists and find it. The first song is called "Canon" by Johann Pachelbel.

"Do you want earbuds?" I ask. "Is this the song with cannons in it?"

"Oh, that. No, this one's older. The one with cannons is a Tchaikovsky song. I don't know the name. And please no ear buds," he says and closes his eyes. "This is good. These are good traveling songs."

I am not sure what he means by traveling—like we haven't been traveling this whole time, my whole life. But he's sick. He looks very bad. His skin is still a green-gray color. I pat him on the shoulder—it's kind of awkward.

"Hey," he says, "you don't have to stay."

But I think that is exactly what he wants. "No," I say. "I want to hear these songs, too."

And we stay like that. The room becomes a pocket of sound full of flowers and violins and sweetness.

After three songs, John-Michael takes a deep (and heavy and hard) breath and says, "Could you leave me with this now?"

"Sure," I tell him, but I hesitate. I really don't know if I should leave. What if something goes wrong while I'm gone?

"Go on," he assures me. "I want to be alone right now."

I pat him on the shoulder again—and yeah, it's a little awkward again—and leave the room. I go through to the bathroom and clean up and start heading forward in the ship. I have to go through John-Michael's room again. He is humming a little, eyes closed. Then I'm out the other side of the room.

I look back through the door at him and call out, "I'll come back later." He doesn't say anything.

In the burned corridor, I inhale the tinge of fire in the air of that room and blow out through my mouth. The music playing from John-Michael's phone sounds tinny from here.

I get back up to the front of the ship with Sergei and the captain. I'm not sure if they've left this area at any time in the past day. I have not been paying attention to them and that part of the ship. They could have gone out on a space walk, started synthing paint, or had a Kraftwork game for all I know.

They look up at me with two sets of tired and red eyes. I guess that answers my question.

I go sit in the co-pilot chair.

"How are you doing, Rosie?" Sergei asks me.

"I'm fine. John-Michael doesn't look so good. But I should ask about you: are you feeling better?"

"Ah," says Sergei and he puffs out his chest. "I get better and better."

I sit and listen to Sergei and the captain go over plans while I check messages. I still have to keep up with the ones from the WSC. It's comforting, I think, what with the messages and timelines and the two voices in the background.

When I finally have gone through all the new notes and information—though I haven't done anything about anything—I watch the way Sergei and the captain interact. Sergei is a mobile person. Always moving and seeming to tease people. The captain is the opposite physically, calm and serious. He's the one with the straightest posture on the ship.

Then I get a com from my dad:

Go check John-Michael. Medibot says he's not breathing.

I jump a little and get out of my seat. "I have to go," I announce. "John-Michael isn't breathing."

Sergei and the captain are behind me and we move quickly through the quarters to John-Michael's room. Dad and Jordan arrive right after us.

I know what John-Michael looks like. I just saw that this morning. It looks like he's dead now, too. Jordan assesses him the same way my dad did for Panchi, with Medibot and by laying hands on him. Jordan's hands don't shake the way my dad's did. He is steady as he goes through the routine.

And here we are, all in one room, the crew of the Grimm Explorer. The captain, Dad, Jordan, Sergei, and me.

There is no one howling for John-Michael. He only wanted to be with Panchi. He would have wanted only to hear her voice, too, maybe. I think.

Chapter 48

It's Friday. Jordan has asked everyone to gather in the galley at 1200 hours. We are going to honor John-Michael and Panchi.

Ghosh-MacFarland would be a pretty good name for a planet, I think. Maybe I will suggest that we re-name Kepler-917. Maybe that is too depressing and a crappy way to name planets. I don't want to name any more planets like this.

Jordan continues to look weak. Sergei continues to look like he's pretending to be well even when he's not. My dad and the captain both continue to look tired.

Jordan starts talking, but I am lost in my own thoughts. Panchi was the sort of person who seemed disengaged with everyone except John-Michael. John-Michael was the sort of person for whom there was only one light, and that was Panchi. It was like he followed where she went and she liked that.

When I tune in to what's being said, Jordan is listing degrees and awards. It sounds a little like a job resume. Nice, I guess.

Maybe someone will say about them that they are in the next room. Maybe someone will say it feels like they could come back at any time. But now that there are going to be four bodies in the launch bay, I'm not sure anyone wants to say that. Can ghosts haunt a spaceship? Are we moving too fast for that?

When Jordan's turn is done, my dad takes the floor.

"I want to share one small thing about Panchi and John-Michael each. And one thing about them together." He looks down at the deck. "Panchi was an introverted woman. But one night back as we all were preparing to leave Earth, we all went out to a karaoke bar. And what did Panchi do? She disappeared into the bathroom for a while and came out with her hair styled like something from the 20th century vids, piled forward, and way, way up high, with strands pulled down for sideburns and everything. She then proceeded to do the most hip-swiveling, arm-swinging rendition of some ancient rock song. It was the most hilarious thing, especially because the rest of the time Panchi was head down in a device, studying, or working, and she always seemed quite serious. She had a good voice." He looks around now, above all our heads. "Now John-Michael was the kind of person who liked to take care of other people. And he used to take his nephews to Washington Ravens football games every year. They'd make a weekend of it. The boys would stay overnight at Panchi and John-Michael's house in D.C., play with the dogs, and eat candy with their uncle. I think the boys loved it. Football was only part of it. John-Michael told me once it was a little slice of heaven." He looks at us, into our faces. "And the thing I want to share about them both is something I think everyone here has seen, but no one has talked about. When you saw them together, you often saw that they were touching the sides of their feet or hands together, like people do when they first fall in love. John-Michael and Panchi did that all the time, especially hanging out in the galley or playing a game or working side-by-side in the project room. I wonder if they thought no one noticed. Or if being seen mattered to them enough to think about being noticed."

When my dad stops talking, everyone stays quiet, barely breathing.

Then the captain adds, "They will be missed."

Chapter 49

I am going to go to bed now—I don't care that it's only 1500 hours. I will pull my blanket over my head. My phone will light up when Ethan Junior sends me things. I will ignore that light. I will turn the phone upside-down. I do not know who or what Panchi was trying to be. I do not know much about any sports team or John-Michael and Panchi's life before they were on board the Grimm Explorer. And I will not look these things up or watch old vids. I will stay in my bunk as long as I can or at least until I stop crying or at least until my face calms down and my feelings can't be seen by everyone. Sometimes I just don't want to be seen.

Chapter 50

I do not feel like just a passenger anymore. Over the past month, I've changed from doing chores, to having a job. I've swapped homework and exercising with duties, projects, homework, and exercising. Although I sometimes feel like I barely know what to do, everyone is expecting me to be able to get up to speed immediately with no time to get used to anything. Zero learning time.

When you are the only kid around, you feel like you should be a part of grown-up culture, but you also feel like you don't understand it, like some crucial parts of it are going over your head.

I am in a very weird place mentally. It feels like I'm the only one in the universe who's going through what I'm going through. Sometimes all I want to do is take care of my dad. Sometimes all I want to do is the work that's being asked of me. Sometimes all I want is for that work to stop. I feel twenty emotions at once and then feel empty. I have no idea how to fix any of it. Even if I could change things, I wouldn't know what I would choose to feel instead.

Dad is so out of it. Here's an example of how disconnected

and moody he is. You tell me if you'd know what to do.

He still sews on Wednesday nights at 2000 hours. It's a date night with no date. I stay far away from him during those times mostly because I feel awkward. But last night was Wednesday night and I thought I should be brave and join him. When I got to the project area, he didn't look at me. So, just as I have been expecting, it was uncomfortable. I sat down and picked up a jumpsuit with a broken hem. I started talking about the farm or something and he just grabbed the cloth from my hand and slapped it down. "Leave that alone," he said. "You don't know what you're doing."

"Okay," I answered. Then I sat there for ten minutes. Both of us were quiet. Then I left. I'm a coward sometimes.

I am a little bit glad for Sergei and Jordan because they are both like uncles to me and I can talk to them without any drama. I think I could even kick them in the shins and they would laugh and it would be okay. I'm not going to kick them in the shins or anything, but if I did, I think they would not get mad. I wish everything was like that.

Chapter 51

It has been four weeks since John-Michael and Panchi died. Everyone left on board the ship is well and healthy now. We feel lonely, though.

This morning, I am on the flight deck. It has become my go-to spot on the ship. Usually someone else is here, but right now I have it to myself. I'm supposed to be doing Government lessons. Yes, I still have schoolwork. But I am really just watching the stars, meteors, and colored lights slip by in the space-dark sky.

In a little while, I'll shake off this feeling and finish my assignment. Then lunch. Then work out. Then work.

Or I will wander through the ship to see what's going on. I get up from the chair, put my devices away and head back, all the way to the farm.

Jordan has redone the food charts a few times now. Practically speaking, there are no restrictions on eating since there are only five people left on board the ship and we have not cut back on growing food yet. But I think Jordan keeps up the practice of preparing food charts in order to try to make sure everyone eats enough and gets the right nutrients, and so on.

Jordan also took over managing all the agriculture modules and most of the work on the farm. Panchi used to do the farm management with occasional help from Sergei. Jordan always liked doing the hands-on work in the farm.

Food from the farm is way more than a supplement to our diet. The nutrients are critical and, really, they are the bulk of what keeps our stomachs full.

"Hey, Jordan," I call out when I get there. Jordan's head pops up from behind a row of hydroponic containers.

"Hey," he says in return. "Are you here to work or to hang out?"

"Hang out, mostly. What are you up to?"

"I'm trying to design a nutrition study."

Jordan starts talking about how—after we get back to Earth—he might continue to focus his studies on nutrition in space during extended flights.

Jordan continues. "I'm trying to see if I can flip the nutrition and health data from the ship into something worth compiling and analysing. I have a lot of it now—not just on you, Rosie, but also the others. Problem is, it's going to be flawed because you're the only one left who is not male and not fully adult and it's hard to generalize about nutrition when a group is this small and limited in diversity."

He's really excited about this, because he continues. "But we do have many, many years of rather exact information about what has been eaten. That is so unusual without putting a sensor in your stomach—and as far as I know people just don't do that much anymore. Alternately, the WSC did not release the crew's genetic registrations to me—so I don't know if any crew member had any unique nutrition needs." He pauses and takes a breath.

While Jordan has been going on and on about each crew member's possible nutrition requirements, I raise my phone and take a shot of the rows of hydroponic growing containers. Along the walls, Jordan has created a mural of farmland. So my image has that in the background. There's a cow and a rooster. I take another picture and do that thing where I make the rows of containers blurry and the farmland mural not-blurry. It's really just a technique of tricking the camera's autofocus. The resulting image is not a particularly inspiring composition or subject even. Maybe it will look better in grayscale, but I doubt it. Not enough contrasts here.

I message Ethan Junior.

Yo, when you get on, ping me. I'm bored.

Ethan Junior responds right away.

hey i'm at lunch

I send this back to him.

Just seeing what's going on. Gave up trying to work on school assignments. Current subject: a U.S. government project on the senators of all the 51 states.

Ethan Junior follows up.

are you going to go to school when you get to earth or what

I actually know the answer to this question.

I'm probably going to finish the HS degree on ship. And after I get back I will mostly be recovering from my life on a spaceship. I will miss seeing you in the marching band at the football games. :-/

And Ethan Junior responds to me like this:

that is for the best
gotta get to pre calc back at u later

It looks like I better get back to my school project now, too. It's a presentation on the gender and racial makeup of U.S. senators and how that relates to (or doesn't relate to) the constituents whom they represent. Pretty standard stuff.

Chapter 52

Writing about it to Ethan Junior made me realize that I want to complete my high school degree soon. Like right now. I think I'm close. I'm sure I'll have to arrange for the long-distance tests. I have gotten through so much of the science and math coursework it's like I'm a college sophomore in those areas. But studying Government, Spanish, English, Health, and things like that has sometimes taken a backseat to the science and math.

I log onto .Xtremity. Mom used to say I have had a weird education because I'll sometimes study one thing for weeks and then switch to something else. It doesn't feel weird to me—I like it.

I send a message to Ms. French, my counselor, and copy Dr. Maney, my school coordinator. To be honest, I almost never engage with Ms. French about anything more than making sure I'm getting enough credits in enough subjects. I deal with Dr. Maney instead.

I'm sure my message is out of the blue to her.

> *Hello! What do I need to do to finish up my high school degree? Thanks!*

Basically, although I think I am very close, I haven't been paying any attention to it lately. Too much going on. Mom was better keeping me focused on my schoolwork.

Ms. French sends this message back.

Rose Marie, on the transcript tool, there's a module that lists the requirements you have fulfilled, the grades you got in them, and the requirements you still have to complete. If you'd like to look over your coursework with me, let's arrange a time. I took a quick peek at your records, so I can tell you that you'll find that you are only 10 credits short of a high school diploma.

At this point you can test out of English 12 and Spanish 4 with just an exam. You finished your social intractive unit requirement, but you have to do projects in addition to taking tests in order to complete Health and Government. There is also a community service requirement you must fulfill.

Would you like to schedule the tests for English and Spanish?

That was fast. I respond to her right away, too:

Yes, I'd like to get the tests out of the way as soon as I can and then we can see about the Health and Government projects. And the community service requirement.

She sends this message back.

I've sent three possible times for each test to your school account. Look them over and let me know which times you'd like to use—or if you'd like to push the dates back on those. Then I'll set them up. For Spanish there is a conversational module and we'll need to have an instructor have a talk with you in Spanish to assess your speaking skills.

I switch to .Xtremity and load up the requirements section. I then log into my full school account for the first time in three months. Ms. French's message is right on top. (And wow, are there a lot of unopened messages in there. It turns out I've missed homecoming and prom. Again. Oh, darn.)

Yes. Thanks. I have everything. I'll let you know.

She replies back to that, wanting to give me a deadline.

Be sure to let me know by the end of the month when to set things up. After that, you might have to wait until next semester. And good luck!

I look at my calendar—which is typically completely empty of anything because, well, why would I use anything like that. All my days would look like this: "Day 1: on spaceship." "Day 2: on spaceship." "Day 3: on spaceship." And so on. But anyway, this means there's nothing to restrict my schedule and no reason to pick one time over another. And so I pick the times for each of these tests that are as late as possible—except for the Spanish conversation evaluation (or whatever that will look like) which would land on the same day as the Government test, so I pick the next latest date for that.

Maybe I can be done with high school in a couple months.

Maybe I can get Spanish credit for having a grandmother who is fluent and a mom who was partly fluent?

Maybe I should go ahead and write up my choices and send them off to Ms. French and Dr. Maney.

Chapter 53

This morning, Ethan Junior asked if I wanted to make a new vid for the channel. At first, I thought it would be too much—I've been pretty busy during the day recently. But it turns out that I don't sleep when I'm supposed to sleep, so I started a new project.

Instead of little animals, I made figures for each one of us on the Grimm Explorer. I did the first scene last night, after Dad crashed, sound asleep and huffing and puffing hard through his nose, on his bunk. (It's not quite the spectacle of snoring that I've seen in recordings.)

The vid starts with the current five of us on the ship. It was easier to start with only five so I wouldn't have to make models of everyone from the start. We're having dinner in the first scene. A birthday dinner.

The second scene, I plan to do tonight. It's a tribute to Panchi and John-Michael and shows them in their room together at the end.

And that is how the rest of the vid is going to go. I'll do the scenes moving backwards in time. I'll show when I got sick while walking around on Finch-Hernandez. I'll show the shuttle with my mom and Jackie tumbling into the dark side of the planet. That is a vision I cannot shake. It visits me often. I'll make the dialog of Mom and Jackie as they go through the process of launching and piloting to the planet for the first manned run. I can probably get the actual recording for that and edit it to fit the vid. I can make sure to cut it down to the sweetest, funniest, nicest parts of their conversation. It will not be hard to show this. They were sweet, funny, and nice people.

The vid will restore the entire population to the Grimm Explorer. And the ending will be my 15th birthday dinner, when we didn't know anything bad could happen and we were joking about sisters and names and magicians and parties.

It will also out me as the girl on the spaceship. The whole world might know I'm the girl on Hurricanes and Rocks. Now the whole world will know that she is THAT particular girl. They might not care.

My working title is "One Month" because that's pretty much the time span it's going to cover. Only about one month. Who am I kidding? That is not a working title. That's just what the title is.

Chapter 54

Hey

I'm alerting Ethan Junior to the fact that I want to talk.

hi

He took three hours to respond, but there he is. I send a message back to him.

I've got a new vid for you.

He takes another hour to get back to me. I think maybe I am interrupting him.

yeah?

I hope he stays up and connected.

Yeah.

I guess he is staying up because I finally get a real response almost right away.

good cause im getting more subscribers and they are gonna
expect more regular posts
we are over 1000 subscribers

Great, I think. Another set of obligations. I am going to avoid thinking about that and just tell him about my project like I wanted to.

I'm doing a longer vid than usual. And more serious. It's a little weird in format. Is that okay?

He responds:

im sure its great ill look at it when it arrives but im sure its great
plus the channel needs more vid
plus i like everything so far
plus it better be great
im picky

I mention the one big thing he should be aware of:

It's set on the spaceship, sooooooo ...
Soooo folks might realize who La Gata is.

His answer shows he doesn't seem to think it matters.

they might not put two and two together?
they might think its some joker making up stories about you all?
all created content is a construct and therefore fiction anyway?

I answer that last one.

Or fiction and reality overlap in the mind of the viewer.
The filmmaker is merely the conduit for the subconscious expression of the psyche. How esoteric of you.

This kind of talk continues for a little while. In the end, we agree to see what happens, for better or worse. I set up the file transfer to his WSC account and watch my phone spin. I think it's a good vid. It's twenty minutes long so I am worried that it's going to be too long for the usual kind of viewership that Hurricanes and Rocks gets. It is what it is.

Chapter 55

Tonight, I'm all set up on the flight deck to study for my high school completion exams. If I'm quiet, I figure there's no reason for them not to let me stay up here with the lights in space for company. I have a phone and a tablet. The tools are open. I'm ready to go.

First, I need to read about the presidential elections and the electoral college of the United States. It's for an essay comparing the electoral college to the popular vote and uses that as a device to show its purpose but also to show where it gives more power to the less populated states.

It turns out the article is not interesting at all. I don't care how many elections were weird because of it. At least six. Maybe I can think of something interesting to say about it in my essay?

Because the article is so not interesting, I am actually relieved when my dad messages me from our quarters.

What's going on?

I respond:

Reading government stuff.

He's right on that.

I was thinking about setting up a game of cribbage or something. You interested?

So I hit the "y" button

And that is answered with silence, so I figure I'll just keep reading my homework.

But Dad shows up, looking weird. His eyes are almost crossed.

"Are you okay, Dad?" I ask.

"No," he says. "You know what I don't like right now? I don't like having my daughter just brush me off."

"What? I don't think I did that?" I say.

"Yes. Yes, you did. You hit that stupid "y" button. It's like a swat. Like, boom, you can't say anything. Too busy. Too unavailable."

"I didn't know you thought that."

"It just irritates me so much. It seems really ... really ... dismissive. Like, slap, end of discussion."

"Okay. Okay. I'll give you real answers from now on."

He sits in the co-pilot seat, head hanging a little.

After a while, I ask, "Is it okay if I use a one-letter answer when I really do mean to brush you off?"

That gets a smile from him. And I'm glad. I really had no idea this bothered him. I haven't really used letters or icons for much with him.

I wonder if he knew Mom and I used to send random pics to each other. The more random the better. I would send her an image of an alligator and a baby chicken. She would send me a whale and a wedge of swiss cheese. I'd send her a snowman. She'd send a lizard. And so on. Maybe all this has to do with her. Did Mom and Dad do that, too? But that's different than one letter abbreviations.

Maybe he just doesn't like those. What I would give for a message with nothing but an egg in it right now.

Chapter 56

Ms. French scheduled my tests in English 12 and Spanish 4 for the dates and times I requested. Dr. Maney organized study sessions for each of those tests. And we all have coordinated on my final projects in Health and Government. I still haven't figured out the community service project.

My project for Health is to create annotated drawings of the human skeleton with an overlay feature that you can activate to show the muscles and organs. The good thing about this is that it is entirely digital. It's due at the end of the month with my Government project. I have an idea to improve the Health project already. Instead of just a drawing of a guy standing and looking straight out of the screen, I think I'll make it animated and show a guy running down a field and hurdling over logs, sleeping dogs, bears (who swipe at him), bicycles, lamp shades, and other assorted items. I'll do it so you can see it as a skeleton or add the muscles to watch them work. Should the dogs and bears be animated skeletons with muscle overlays? I might not have time for that. And people might not realize what they are.

My Government project is to organize a presentation comparing the government of the United States of America with other governments in the world. I've got the work I did on the Congress from before—the one comparing the demographics of the elected representatives to their constituents. I plan to start by expanding that old project to an analysis of all the senators and congresspeople of all 51 of the United States of America showing which of the three parties they belong to and what place they're representing in order of their entry into the union, starting with Delaware (the first state to sign the declaration of independence) and ending with Puerto Rico (which attained statehood only after over 150 years of being a territory). Then, I'm doing a survey of several other governments for a big comparison. So: India, Russia, Canada vs. the U.S. If I think about it as data analysis, maybe it will seem more interesting to me. Yeah, data analysis will totally spice things up for me. Maybe I'll choose a different country than Russia—they've got a complicated history. Maybe Mexico? Maybe Britain?

My other idea for this project was an analysis on the effects of sea level rise on the economic powers of small coastal nations. But that project would require a vast pile of data. So government comparisons it is!

Chapter 57

rosie rosie
rosie
!!!!

Ethan Junior is hitting up my phone. You know it's got
to be big because this is 6 a.m. Florida-time (0600 hours).
I'd be less surprised if he was connecting up from Moscow-
time (which would be 3 p.m. right now) or California time
(which would be 3 a.m.). He continues:

5000000 views rosie!!! 5000000!

I think I know what he's talking about, but I am not
sure. Yes, this early, it's got to be big, but it sounds like
he's got to be talking about something on Hurricanes and
Rocks. 5,000,000 views sounds like rock-star range, if
that's what it is. I respond:

For one of your vids on the channel, dude?

And he is right back to me with this:

rosie rosie its for YOUR vid on OUR channel

For my vid? I have no real response. I am actually
focused on the fact that I don't think I've ever seen Ethan
Junior message anything with a capital letter, much less a

whole word of caps. Here's me:

For MY vid? The backwards one? One Month?

Here's him:

yes that one and all the other vids on hurricanes and rocks
are getting more hits too - but thats the one behind it all.

Huh. I made the backwards vid because I had to act it out that way. I had to show everything slide back to a previous, happier time. I once read a book like that and it seemed to be a good way to fill up the earlier time with the feelings of the later time. Like memory does. Something like that.

And it was easier to make only five characters to start with, to be honest.

Here's me tapping out a message to Ethan Junior again:

Let's continue talking on vid chat. I want to see the stats for
myself, first. See you there in an hour.

We connect again over on the backend of the channel (with the WSC connect boost) at around 0730 hours. At this point, I have gotten onto the channel admin area and have looked at all the stats for my vid (over 5,500,000 views by now) and scroll through the other posts. The subscribers are up to 4,000 and rising.

We talk about scheduling stuff. He says he can make daily vids—people will be expecting regular content. But can I pick up the pace? I am not sure.

We are spending an unprecedented amount of time on the live vid connection. I think Dad is letting me use it because I'm more excited about going viral than I have been about school or anything else in a long time. I won't challenge him on that.

I tell Ethan Junior I can do a vid right now about the human skeletal system and the muscular system. "Something funny or what?" he asks.

"Oh, it'll be funny," I say. "I think I'll sing the song my mom sang to me for exercising. You know, the one with the movements. The ribs climb day and night, day and night."

"Uh, not sure if that's funny. Send it if it works out," he adds.

"Okay, okay, or I'll pick a historical figure and make a mock monolog," I say. "I'll have Emily Dickinson or Barack Obama swearing up a storm or something."

"There's something like that already for both of those guys, but you can find other people to do that with. I think I'll complain about the weather in Florida every day—no matter what," he says.

"Yes! That's good," I tell him.

Finally he says, "Look, I think you should do whatever you're feeling. I'll do the daily stuff. That's the channel. Hurricanes and Rocks. Though I think we got it wrong—you're the once-in a-while great hurricanes and I'm the daily rocks."

After many hours of brainstorming ideas, I've got a couple that I want to work on besides cursing historical figures. And so does Ethan Junior—the daily weather will be a great standard vid. He's such a goof.

I feel so good about this. Sure, it's weird that a vid about my life is getting that much attention. It might be short-lived. It might have something to do with my being the only kid in space. But I'm feeling good with how I expressed it.

Chapter 58

It's getting to be dinnertime and Sergei and I are on the flight deck. I'm curled up with a full-size laptop in the co-pilot's seat working on my Health project for school. Sergei is sitting up and working in the pilot's seat. I alternate between looking out the window panels at the stars and the Milky Way which is toward Earth's solar system—we can now identify it visually—and checking the navigation routines and futzing with my project.

Sergei is working on the final procedures for coming into Earth, which is in three months.

Yep, this feels more like hanging out than it feels like work. But we are, in fact, working.

Sergei says he has a message from his mom, who lives in Moscow.

"It's like almost 0200 hours there? Right?" I ask.

"Yep, she says she can't sleep," he replies. "She plays old tv vids to keep herself company or she sends notes to her kids."

"Is that a good thing or not?"

"Let us see," he says while he messages her back. "She

is excited for my re-entry into Earth's atmosphere. Here we are. Her official answer. She says she likes having all her kids breathing and safely on Earth. And she adds lots of smiles to her answer."

"Did you know," Sergei continues. "I spent one whole year on Moscow-time?"

I turn my attention from the laptop.

"You were small. Very little. I was home-sick and thought living like that would be like honoring home. I had more voice conversations with family during that year. But it ended up being hard to maintain. Felt like midnight all day. I was lonely in a different way. And one day when it was night for you and morning for me, you got out of your bunk—you were like five and missing two front teeth—and found me eating. We had snacks and I put you back in bed. 'Let's not make this regular!' I insisted. 'You need sleep!'"

"I remember that," I say, while smiling. "I thought you were joking, but also serious."

"I was joking, but also serious," he agrees. "Well, you are not so small now. And Earth is closer every day."

"Hey, I'm done with this health project for now. But I'm going to check the channel," I change the subject. This is so I don't have to have a conversation about not being little anymore which will most likely lead to a conversation about not being grown up yet.

"All right. I like company," he answers.

On our channel, Ethan Junior and I are up to 30,000 subscribers.

I've added a couple long vids—or at least they're longer-than-our-usual vids. One of them is another backwards story—more playful than the last vid like that. It's about a medieval knight. It starts with him about to joust with a rival and drifts backwards through battles, some religious festivals, flirting with a lady fair, his training as a knight, his time as a squire and a page. I put in an increasing number of pratfalls and embarrassing events as he gets younger. Then I had the ending scene jump back to the joust which he loses and we finish the vid with him staring up at the sky, on his back, in the mud. That ending felt like a big, artistic decision. For me anyway.

"Our stats are up," I tell Sergei. "We've got even more subscribers."

"That is pretty hot stuff considering it's mostly vids about Florida weather," says Sergei.

"Ha. Ha. But yeah, that's true. And Ethan Junior yells a lot. He's great to watch. I've seen him take off his shirt like 12 times."

"He shows his pale, skinny boy chest?" asks Sergei.

"Yes, he shows his pale, skinny boy chest."

I start looking around and hitting the WSC channel. They've got mostly promotional and historical vids on there. They release stuff from the archives all the time.

But their top hit-getting piece of content is something new and not really a vid. And I recognize it.

It's a slideshow of images. My images. But these are the ones I took after I swapped my devices out after the first hacks. Images of the ship, of the samples, of the bunk. And it's on the official WSC site.

They didn't ever ask me about this. Is this okay? Can they do that? Was the hacker someone from within the organization?

"Sergei," I say. "I think I found a problem."

"With your vids?"

"No. You remember how I was hacked and my image files from my phone and the ship's network were downloaded somewhere? There was that book people could buy?"

"Yes. Right after John-Michael's direct oobi sync line caught fire."

"I just found images I took after those were hacked, and now they are in a slideshow vid on the WSC channel. Very weird."

He says, "Why would they turn up there? I would expect

something like that to pop up on an anonymous channel. You should take it up with WSC."

"Yeah. But I don't know who to talk to or how this happened or what is going on," I say. "Dad." I use the com. "Dad. I think I'm going to need some help on something."

My face feels hot. I feel embarrassed. Why do I feel embarrassed? Yuck. I just don't want to be involved in things that are wrong or stolen. Ugh. If this feeling was a shirt, I would take it off immediately.

Honestly, I don't really mind my images going out there into the world. I put stuff on Hurricanes and Rocks all the time. Maybe I just want credit. Maybe I just want to know why that happened. Why didn't they talk to me or ask?

On the other hand, now that this is happening on the WSC channel, it means the hack might have had something to do with them.

"Let me see," asks Sergei.

I re-start the vid of the images. The timer shows that it's about an hour long. That is really long. Who would sit and watch still images for an hour? It begins with a series of images I took from the flight deck that were basically the same shot in different spectra. So it shows a standard image, followed by an infrared image, followed by ultraviolet.

I let Sergei watch the vid. He leans forward, sometimes pausing the playback. He's saying, "These are interesting," as my dad arrives up front with us.

Dad starts watching the vid, too, as I repeat to him that those are my images (which is obvious) and that they are more recent than the hack (also obvious). "I see. I can tell they're yours," says Dad. "But I never really watched them in a row before."

"Should I do anything?" I ask.

"I think I'll send some questions to people at WSC. They know about the hack and the book. Jorge Mahon was supposed to follow up with Ethan O'Neil about it. I never heard and never checked on it. But I know I wasn't thinking that it came from inside the WSC. That would explain a lot."

"What would it explain?" I feel like an idiot for not understanding my dad's thinking.

"You know, with access to the WSC system and maybe some of the software, it would be a lot easier to get to you and past some of the security which focuses on malware and virus-ware originating from outside the WSC. And they would have been more likely to have access to the servers that are connected to the interstellar communications systems."

"Oh."

"That's the plan, honey," says Dad. "I feel better after seeing this. I think it makes more sense."

Chapter 59

By breakfast-time the next day, my dad has an answer. He calls me and the captain back to the project room.

"Here it is. The answer you've been waiting for regarding the hack of Rose Marie's devices. It turns out to be a combination of graft and oversight and laziness," starts Dad.

"What is that supposed to mean?" I blurt out.

"Let him continue," says the captain.

"Someone was trying to make a buck." Dad opens something on his phone without showing us, probably to check notes or a message. "A guy by the name of Ed Danzer set up the hack while he was working for the WSC. He pulled the files off a server connected to the communications system."

"Why did he stop?" I ask.

"He stopped because he got fired for something unrelated—which is an interesting story, but unrelated. So he had the files, got fired, then set up the anonymous publication of that book. He did make some money off that. A few hundred thousand dollars. Not sure if that's enough to make up for ruining a reputation, but there you go."

"But that doesn't explain these pictures," says the captain.

"Right. I'm talking with one of WSC's lawyers about this, but it's where the oversight and laziness parts come in and where WSC has more explaining to do. It turns out that after Danzer left, the hidden tool on the WSC network was still in place and copying any images and vids you sent to a second WSC server. They were discovered when the file sizes were noticed in a routine audit of bandwidth and storage use. Basically, they were starting to take up a lot of room. Since part of the tool was hiding on the WSC side, it didn't matter how many times you changed devices or accounts. Even with a clean phone, it would keep happening. Once the files were found, the geniuses in the WSC communications department thought that the images would be great promotional material for the organization. And they didn't ask you, or tell you, because they didn't think they had to ask you or tell you about it. The files were on WSC servers and they figured that was all the ownership or permission they needed. Well, 'figured' is too strong a word. I think they probably didn't 'figure' or think about it at all," concludes my dad.

"What's going to happen now?" I ask.

"What do you want to happen?" responds the captain.

"They can use them. It is a WSC mission, of course. But can I ask them to put my name on it? Can they belong to me in some way instead of belonging to the WSC? And can they not sell anything or make a book or anything without my permission? Maybe I should get part of any sales, if any sales actually happen. I mean I don't care about money. And I am pretty sure there isn't much money to be made. But that guy Ed Danzer made something."

"It will be simplest to do that. Any legal action would probably cost more than it's worth," says Dad.

"As long as they don't use any of the vids—those are out

there on our channel. It would be totally wrong to put them on one of the WSC channels," I say.

"Any legal action will get plenty of media attention," says the captain. "But let's give WSC a chance to issue a statement to reduce the damage to their reputation. And I'm not sure if it's worth it to them to go after your creative work."

"Okay. So that's a plan?" says Dad.

"Yes," says the captain. "Is that acceptable, Rosie?"

"Yes, I think so," I agree.

Dad repeats the plan—I think for my benefit. "I'll contact the communications, PR, and legal departments on their roles in this. Get some kind of ongoing agreement based on your requests, Rosie. I'll also tell them they can't use any of the creative vids—which they haven't yet. I'd imagine that the promotional value of the images improves if they put your name on it. I'll ask legal for advice on what to do about Ed Danzer."

"Dad, is that DeeDee's father?" I ask.

"Who is DeeDee?"

"She was a friend who came to that Kraftwork server birthday party," I tell him. "Her last name was Danzer, too. We didn't talk a lot, or even much. But her dad used to work for the WSC."

"Maybe so, maybe so," says my dad. "It supports the special interest in you. But it doesn't connect to anything in a solid way. I'll send a message to them about that, too."

"Why did he get fired?" I ask.

"Oh, he was trying to sell some of the newly developed but not-yet-patented tech on a social media site."

"A cad," says the captain.

"A cad," agrees my father.

Chapter 60

It's been a long time coming. I've been planning and reviewing material for finishing school for, it seems, ever. I think the entire ship is tired of me talking about it. So, today and tomorrow, finally, actually, and at last, I will get to take my English 12 and my Spanish 4 equivalency tests.

I'm pretty confident I'll ace them. My Spanish lessons have been a way to reinforce what my mom taught me. And no, I don't think it's too unfair to take a language your mother's parents are fluent in. I am only classroom fluent. I'm not sure how I would fare if I had to get by with Spanish only. I think I wouldn't get too far past, "¿Hablas español?" The other person would for sure start talking and using slang and I would be totally lost.

Maybe they should have fixed me up with another pen-pal who mainly speaks Spanish. Maybe. I'm glad for the friends that I have. Too bad Ethan Junior takes Chinese in school.

So instead of studying Spanish by having some kind of pen-pal relationship with a native Spanish speaker, I've spent a lot of time lately listening to Spanish-language shows. Sometimes I even think in Spanish. Sometimes. For about two words at a time. Sometimes three.

And all those lessons and recordings and shows are coming together tomorrow for my test.

The first test, the English 12 equivalency, is going to happen whenever I connect up to the system and start it. I have a window of five hours to start it and the test itself is supposed to be three hours long.

After that, I'll immerse myself in the Spanish 4 prep until the test for it tomorrow—I am way more nervous about that test. Maybe I should have scheduled that one first to focus on it more? But then I would have ignored the English 12 test completely. This is probably the best way for me.

Later, I will know if it's "probably" the best way for me or "actually" the best way for me.

Chapter 61

I slept with my phone and the outline of it is impressed into my skin. Last night, I hooked my ears up to an ambient music channel featuring post-post-post-rock. It's what you get when you look for "spacey" music. And yeah, it does go well with the hum of the spaceship. Of course, all the music on board the Grimm Explorer is, by virtue of being played on a spaceship, "spacey." I listen to it with my space ears in my space bunk.

This morning, peeling my phone from the skin on my side and lifting my blanket off my head, I look up first (same smooth curve of gray), and listen for my dad who seems to be already out of the room. The alerts on the phone show a few midnight notes from Ethan Junior asking if I've watched any of the new Homestuck remakes and if I liked them. (Not yet and I don't know.)

Also, there's a message from Ms. French of the Florida school system. Ah. So this is it. My test scores are in.

I hear my heartbeat thudding in my ears—and they feel full of blood. I feel vulnerable for some reason. Whatever it is, has already happened. Deep breath. I open her message

THE EXPERIMENT KNOWN AS ROSE MARIE HERNANDEZ WILLIAMSON

and see my results.

English 12 - Pass. Grade B+
Spanish 4 - Pass. Grade A+
Government - Pass. Grade B
Health - Pass. Grade A+ (comments available)

This means I can apply for my degree and move on from high school—to what, I'm not quite sure. But I can move on.

I look at the comments on my project for Health. They are effusive and I can barely read them. "Beautifully drawn." "Gorgeous concept." "Great sense of humor." "Permission to use in course work for other students." Okay, now I feel embarrassed for some reason. I better talk to Dad about giving it to them for future coursework.

I message my dad from my bunk:

Three guesses: guess who just passed her English, Spanish, Government, and Health tests (and projects) and can apply for her high school degree?

My dad sends something right back:

I'm so proud of you! <3

He actually made the heart with a carat and a three. Cute. Then he adds:

Hang on a sec. I'll be right there. You in our quarters?

Dad arrives just as I'm sending the full word "yes" in a message.

"Honey! This is really great," says Dad.

"I am pretty happy. The grades were not terrible either," I tell him. "But I have to ask you about the Health project."

"What is it?"

"They want to use it as part of the tools available for other students. Should I let them?"

"Do you want to keep it? What are they going to do with it? Are they going to sell it?" Dad is apparently the one with the questions. "You know," my dad continues, "I showed Sergei some of the drawings and he was wowed. Especially the layers that show the muscle groups."

"Yeah, I gotta fix those." I say.

"You have to fix those? I don't know, but I'm impressed with what they look like now and how focused you were on getting the work exactly right. I would say you should ask Ms. French what the school is planning to do with them, who would use them—that kind of thing. Definitely make sure you are credited with the work. Maybe I'm just thinking about that because of your photography at the WSC." He goes back to gushing. (I go back to rolling my eyes and feeling sheepish.) "Wow. I mean really, I could not have done this."

"But I made that out of nothing."

"You made it with hard work—work that—I said this already—I couldn't even do. And people know who you are—they might be able to leverage your name as a way to get other students to study more. A lot of good could come from this."

"You know, the WSC didn't even check with me before putting those images out there. At least they're asking me first, right?" This feels like a much better situation.

"Okay, now. Is Ms. French or Dr. Maney going to help you with the degree application? Do you know what else you need?"

"I still need a community project," I answer Dad's second question first. "But I'll message Ms. French and Dr. Maney to double-check on everything and see what they're supposed to do and what I'm supposed to do." I pause. "Dad, do you think if I made the biology project available to all students everywhere for free, that could count as a community project? I think I could say something like, no one can take money for it. Or it has to be free. Or everyone and anyone can use it."

"Rosie, that's a great idea! Let's set up a conversation with Ms. French and Dr. Maney to propose that and review your credits and everything. I could see if there's a special way to license it for everyone to use, but that also doesn't let anyone make a profit off of it." He stops, then asks a question that might have come from my mom. "Do you want to talk about college with them, too?"

"No."

"All right. But you could convert some of your schoolwork into a few credits with the University of Florida. It might be simplest to go with them."

"Does it matter?"

"Yes. But I'm thinking we can postpone any decisions till after we get back to Earth. You can plan and apply then. Maybe we can figure it out during the recovery phase. The recovery phase could possibly throw a wrench into a lot of things."

"Yeah, the recovery phase." Yeah, that. That's going to be at least a year of physical therapy. I am not looking forward to it.

"Okay, you check .Xtremity to make sure we're not missing anything obvious. I'll set something up with Ms. French and Dr. Maney. Deal?"

"Deal."

Chapter 62

Earlier today, Dad set up an official live cam meeting with Ms. French and Dr. Maney. It went slower than I thought it would. We had to go over every credit and grade. But I can tell you about it pretty quickly.

First, the four of us reviewed my electronic transcript for completion of credits and passing grades. Then Ms. French made a preliminary acceptance of my proposal for the community project—turning my biology project into a licensed but free and connected tool available for all students, to be maintained by the state of Florida Department of Education. Once she gets final approval for that from the administration of the high school, we can submit the application for a high school degree. She asked if I wanted to meet with a college counselor on anything. I didn't.

We are two steps closer to my being done with my secondary education. After that, I have no idea what's going to happen and I'm sure my life will be completely different in a way I have no way to predict. Am I ready? Not sure.

Chapter 63

I'm in the galley, spreading fruit gel on a cracker. I lick off the gel and remember eating snacks with my mom. Slurping the water and fruit gel, I taste the two textures and flavors mixing in my mouth. I take a sip of water from the container now and it combines on my tongue with my food—the sugar sweet taste pierces the salty taste which turns around and sharpens the sweet taste again.

She used to give me the inside leaves of lettuce like it was the best treat in the universe. Would it be too obvious to say that—while I thought it was the worst treat in the universe at the time—I now know that she was right? She was right because it was something she loved and wanted to give away to me.

It's been nine months that she has been gone. I have made movies and seen one of them get a lot of attention. And she is still gone. I have lost friends and shipmates and she is still gone. My images were released as a result of theft and neglect. And she is still gone. I got my high school degree and she is gone.

Whatever was normal before, the way we slept and ate

and studied and worked—all that is gone, too. I sleep and eat and study and work in a universe without her. That is what's normal now and I hate it. I hate that "mother" will from here on out equal gone, missing, deceased. It's like there will be some kind of asterisk beside our relationship. That asterisk will also be beside my relationship with my dad. Her absence changes everything and is a big shape in my life.

Fruit gel is not supposed to be so bitter, is it?

Chapter 64

I have not yet opened my eyes this morning. Instead I am as usual cataloging the sounds: the buzz-rush of the air system, the rustle of my blanket (which is like the shush of clothes against a chair on the flight deck), Dad's heavy breathing. Today, this inventory of sound is as complete as can be. So, my eyes open, but I put my blanket over my head and pull my phone under it as my space fills with the heat of my exhaled breath. I send a message to Ethan Junior:

> *Hola*

And he is right there.

> *hey lo*

I send him a link to my newly-hosted and available biology project.

> *How do you like that? It's going to count for my community project for graduation. And it's good thing too, because I was not sure what I was going to do for that from here.*

Ethan Junior writes back.

> *i would have been no help - i plan to volunteer with clean up crews after the next hurricane. they say you get to pick*

up trash and like 100 year old plastic grocery bags

My response:

That sounds like a great idea to me. Do you think you can grab a vid of that for our channel? I think it'd be perfect. Especially with some kind of rant overlaid.

Ethan Junior:

it would be - i'll ask

Me:

Speaking of the channel - they don't seem to have figured out who I am. Do you think we should tell them?

Ethan Junior:

we'd get a lot of attention for that

Me:

Better us than WSC or some guy named Ed.

Ethan Junior:

some guy named ed?

Me:

Yeah, you remember DeeDee from 5th grade? That's her dad. And he's the one who set up the hack last year from inside the WSC. Turns out he made a bunch of money. We got WSC to send out something to make him stop using the material though.

Ethan Junior:

when did that happen?

Me:

Last week

Ethan Junior:

could be in the news but maybe not

Me:

I don't know if anyone cares.
I think we're ready to be known for ourselves. Yeah? Follow early days pioneers on YouTube to legitimate content and vid making careers.

Ethan Junior:

tone it down. we are not living the dream yet. most of those guys went nowhere - some were jokes in the end -

only a few channels worked

Me:

We could be legitimate. You didn't really want to go to college did you?

Ethan Junior

omg rosie i am barely thinking about college - my friends who are seniors are tho wow are they stressed out

Me:

We have a good thing going with the vids and everything. And I'm scared about being on Earth.

Ethan Junior:

it'll be alright - i'm gonna visit you in the recovery place when you are trying to adjust to earth - is everyone on the ship wearing weight suits yet

Me:

For the gravity? Yeah. We should do that more.

Ethan Junior:

i should do that.

Me:

I think the scrawny chest is really working for you, buddy.

Ethan Junior:

it's almost three months till you're here - still time for a lot of vids - course we maybe should say who you are and make a big deal about that before you get here - that attention would be enough to last through the next year or two

Me:

That's not a bad idea. There's going to be some serious down time for me/us after we get to Earth.

At this point the blanket is off my head and I'm lying on my back with my phone in front of me. I switch on the fan on the air vent behind my head, it starts at half speed, and then it seems to fail. I turn it off and on again. There. It's nice to have a little breeze.

Chapter 65

It used to be Panchi and Jordan who took care of the farm—Sergei and John-Michael would help sometimes. Now, Jordan asks everyone to pitch in. So I'm not surprised when he coms me to harvest some veggies.

When I walk into the farm, I pause, looking for Jordan.

Today the grow lights are a checkerboard of purple, pink, and yellow. I'm not sure what part of the farm plan this configuration of lights is, but I'm sure Jordan has something specific in mind.

Jordan is playing music. I bet you anything he's tracking the performance of the plants under different kinds of music as well as different color lights. Today's musical track is some old blue music.

I start by asking about it—you can always start a conversation with Jordan by asking about music. I call out to him, "What's this playing?"

A whole four-by-four array of the lights dims and flickers.

"Damn these lights." His voice comes from behind a bank of growing containers. "It's Buddy Guy. Came out around the millennium. 'Sweet Tea'. Here—this is my favorite track. 'Done Got Old'—I think I know what it's saying, but I also don't know what it's saying. You know what? I'm not sure if maybe we'll play something else while you're here."

"It's blue, yes?" I say.

"Blue? Oh, yeah, no. It's 'the blues.' With an ess."

He takes off his gloves and moves to his phone, which is resting on the side of one of the containers. He scrolls around and scrolls around. "Okay, here. You liked this one as a little kid," he says and he pops a button. "It's Dave Brubeck, 'Take Five'. Very popular mid-twentieth century."

Yeah, I know this one. It seems upbeat and full of energy. I feel like I'm going to cry because most of the time I don't feel this upbeat and I worry that I never will. It feels like someone bopping up and down a city street. All I ever do is move back and forth, pacing along the same path right down the middle of the ship. We are in the belly of the space worm, the Grimm Explorer, moving FTL toward Earth.

"You can start with the ... Hey? What's going on?" says Jordan.

I can't ever hide my feelings, can I? "I'm just feeling weird and I think I want to hear something louder and harder."

"Ah," responds Jordan. "Come over here." He pulls out his hammock-style chairs. "Have a seat. I already know the hard stuff isn't good for the plants. They like it mellow and groovy. You want to talk about it?"

"No," I say.

"Then we'll just sit here. Hang on. I'll be right back."

I sit in the hammock seat and ponder the colored grow lights and the rows of green leaves while Jordan disappears down toward the galley.

When Jordan comes back, he announces, "We don't drink this much on board, but I think this is the perfect time." Then he hands me a cold container of transparent brown liquid.

"What's this?" I ask.

"It's iced tea. No sugar, though. It's not sweet tea. We're just going to sit here and chill out a while. The harvest can wait."

We sit through about two minutes of music and cold tea. It feels starchy and bitter and sweet all at once. Tart. I agree with whoever wanted to make it sweet tea rather than just, you know, tea.

Then I say, "I'm scared about Earth. Being on Earth. All the people. If I can take it."

"You want to prepare for it?" Jordan offers.

"I'm doing everything I'm supposed to do."

"Yeah, you have all the exercises? You can wear a weight suit more?"

"That's not it. Getting to Earth—it's going to be like everything is different. I don't know. It's not about the exercises. I don't know what all I'm going to need to do."

"I can't tell you anymore of what to do, hon, but can I encourage you to live in the moment a little more? Here, we're going to switch to some Branford Marsalis—also a guy making music around the millennium—younger than Buddy Guy. And you're going to pick dill and potatoes. And that's all that's going to happen for the next hour. You can talk—or not talk—the whole time."

I don't know if he understands how overwhelmed I'm feeling, but this is his prescription for me and I'll follow it. "Okay," I tell Jordan and we put on gloves and get to work under pink, purple, and yellow grow lights while some pretty horn music comes on. It sounds like a yellow butterfly.

Chapter 66

It's a birthday today. Jordan's. June 24, 2118. I think he's 50 today. That seems like an incredible age. Half a century. It is hard to believe.

My dad and Sergei are in charge of the dinner tonight—it's their turn on the rotation.

I've got a plan for what I'm going to do for the birthday tonight. But that is hours away. For now, I scroll through the various news and social feeds. I check the channel, watch Ethan Junior complain about a day that—in the background—looks like a sunny, grassy day. He's getting really good at ranting. "It's hot," he says. "Surprise," he says.

Part of the reason I check so many feeds is to look for my stuff, but I don't see anything interesting (or scary or stolen) today. On WSC's feed, they're mostly posting about the Mars colony. It's the 50th anniversary. Or rather, they started building the colony 50 years ago today. Maybe they should count the anniversary as when they finished it. But you could argue for counting the anniversary from today because it is true that a human has been living there since

June 24, 2068—the same day that Jordan was born. The press release vid shows a clip of the heavy lift rockets they used when it first got started. Mars has been popular for a long time. Mars versus Venus. Little green men. The red planet. (Just like Finch-Hernandez is red.)

My mind is more on the stories that are going to happen tonight at Jordan's party. Once again, I'm going to feel like I don't have anything to add.

So, for today, instead of trying to come up with a story (because I don't have any stories), I am going to take all the pictures I have of him and pick out like 30 of the best for a slideshow. (Is that too many?)

I should add music, so I check to see what his favorite song is. Well, maybe it's not going to be his favorite song, but it is going to be his most played song. Hopefully, that is a good sign that he likes it. The counter on his playlist says he's played John Coltrane's "Acknowledgement" 3,456 times. (3,456? Oh, wow. I might have to send him some links to new stuff.) I play the song. It starts out sounding like morning to me and then it escalates. I think this song gets a little raucous for a slideshow, but what do I know?

I drop the music behind the slideshow of pictures I'm building. I add a few images of the farm, and some wording. "Happy birthday," "Wow, you're old," "Get Off of My Lawn", and "Farmer Banks"—I put those last two phrases on two different pictures of him sitting in a chair at the farm with a container of something in his hand. I add an image of a horse to another picture of the farm. I hope he likes it. I hope he knows I'm joking (kind of) about being old.

I finish this up just before 1800 hours rolls around. So I grab a tablet for the slideshow display and head for the galley. Dad and Sergei have it all set up. There's not much in the decoration department, but the food is arranged nicely.

Sergei greets me first. "Hey, Rosie."

"Hi," I answer.

"Honey, can you get the cucumbers?" Dad asks.

I pull them from the cold storage. They're skinned and sliced up in a bowl.

"Put some salt and dill on them," says Dad.

"Got it," I say and proceed with adding spices to the cold veggies. While I'm doing that, I ask, "Can I setup my slideshow?"

"Wait. What?" says Dad.

"Can I setup my slideshow?" I repeat.

"For Jordan?" Dad asks.

"Yep. I took some of his most played music," I answer. "And I put it in the background of a slideshow of pictures I've taken."

"Sounds nice," says Sergei.

"It is nice," I agree.

"Uh, okay. Here, prop the tablet up over here and, uh, we'll run it on a loop," says Dad. "We'll keep the music low so we can talk."

I think this means my presentation is background noise. But okay. I set up the tablet and start it running.

The captain and Jordan arrive and we settle in.

Dad's got the music set really low. Jordan starts scooping the cucumbers out of the bowl for himself.

The captain is the one to begin telling the stories. He says, "I like a rainy morning. Everything seems to slow down. The smell of the street changes to something cleaner. You can hear the rain move through the underground drains and sewers, a creek running under the traffic. When Jack and I were first married, we'd get up early, like 5:30 in the morning and go out walking. I think I liked it best when it was still dark as night at that time."

"Wasn't it always dark at that time?" I ask.

"During the summers, it was light," he answers. "But let me finish before we get off track about the shifting sunrises and sunsets."

Okay, I think, but it's going to bug me. I am going to

think more about how Earth-side sunrises and sunsets work than his story.

"Uh, so, like I said, we'd get up early, even when it snowed. It got so we didn't talk at all. It was peaceful. The sunrise colors always different. I plan to do that again when we get back."

All of us get quiet. I think the captain is going to be more lonely when he gets to Earth. I think he wants to lean into that loneliness and the memories of his wife. What I mean is, some people try to avoid feeling lonely; the captain is not one of those people.

"This song makes me think of mornings," says my dad.

"Me too," I add. "And afternoons." Both of those times look pretty much the same to me, but no one seems to notice. And I will stand by my sentiment. This song does feel like both mornings as well as afternoons.

The five of us sit and watch the pictures go by of Jordan in various places on the ship. There are some chuckles at the funny slides. They all seem to like having the slideshow play during the meal. I'll take that as a success.

Chapter 67

It's July 4th in Florida, USA. So it's July 4th on board the ship. We haven't planned anything for this. That used to be something Jackie and my mom did. They'd devise something for Earth-side U.S. holidays. Sometimes decorations. Sometimes some kind of festive meal. This year, there has been none of that.

Maybe since I thought of it, I should do something about it? I was behind the birthday slideshow for Jordan. Do I want to get behind this as well? Maybe I'll just keep my head down and not say anything.

Instead, I go looking for my dad. I find him near the launch deck at the very back of the ship. I want to ask him if he wants me to make a meal for him. I think he hasn't been eating.

I've been on my own for that lately. Food is hard. Mom, Dad, and I shared so many conversations and jokes over food. Mom told me that with a kid, she felt like making a dinner together every day was more important. Clearly, Dad has let go of that. And that's okay. I'm old enough to get my own sustenance together. Most of the things we eat, I've had and prepared more than 6,502 times (approximately). Still, I'm tired of eating alone all the time. Maybe he is, too.

And maybe a lunch won't feel so much like something we should have Mom around for.

Dad has the wall beside the controls of the launch bay open, with a panel of wires pulled out. He also has one of the floor panels open—you can see some of the big magnets under there that make our gravity.

"Hi. What are you up to, Dad?" I ask.

"Hey, girly," he replies. "I'm trying to replace some wiring. Some of this stuff is no longer working and I'm checking up on it."

"Shouldn't that have been set up to last the whole mission?"

"Yeah, but we're near the end, and sometimes there's no accounting for how things perform over more than 16 years."

"Want some lunch or something?"

"I've got to keep at this. Maybe later?"

"What if I bring you something? Like something you can eat with your hands?"

"Okay. That's good. Thanks."

I go and bring him some carrots and some flat bread. I figure that's easy to pick up and eat while working. Hopefully it's not too bland or messy—though I'm not sure if he'll notice either way.

I tell him lunch is right there. He grunts back at me and keeps working. I leave him to his work and head to the project room.

I think I'm going to make another stop-motion movie. This one is going to be really simple. It will have a dad cat and a girl cat. They will walk around on a beach. I'll make a horse gallop by. I'll have the cat family stand in the cold water and have the water and sand swirl around their ankles with each wave. They will race each other up and down the beach. Mostly they will talk about the things I know most about—which, by the way, is not sand, oceans, and beaches, but stars, rocky deserted planets, and potatoes grown in tanks.

I first make all the characters, two little cats—one cat smaller than the other cat—and a horse. And two sand crabs. The sand crabs look like blobs. I know I'm not going to get a lot of detail out of tin foil, so I'll have to rely on dialog to put them into context. Then I make the facade of a castle for them to look at on the distant, foggy horizon. I won't need more than one side of it.

I have watched a plain vid of small waves washing up on sand 3,602 times. I have watched another vid of waves washing around feet 2,712 times. I really hope I can get that feeling right.

When I have the scenery and characters made, it's almost dinnertime. So I go check on Dad. He's putting away the electrical panel as I get there.

"Hi, Dad," I say.

"Oh, honey, hi," he responds.

"How about I clean up for you?"

"Thanks. I'll get the tools."

"No, I mean the lunch you didn't eat." I look at the plate on the floor.

"I wasn't very hungry, but I did appreciate you bringing it to me."

"That's okay. But you must be hungry now. I'll make you something in the galley and I won't take 'no' for an answer."

"All right, Rosie. I'm going to go lie down for a bit. Come get me when dinner's ready."

Dad drops me off at the galley, where Jordan and Sergei are finishing a meal of pancakes, fruit, and lettuce.

"That looks good," says Dad.

"I'll make that for you, yeah?" I ask.

"Good, good," says Dad as he moves through the doorway of the galley toward our quarters.

"They're very tasty," says Sergei. "Want some company while you make your dinners?"

Jordan adds, "Sergei and I would love to watch you cook while providing fascinating conversation."

"I have a question for you guys anyway," I say. "I'm making a little movie and I have a dad character and a daughter character. Would either one of you like to be the dad?"

"I would love to be one of your voice actors!" states Sergei.

But Jordan counters him. "I think you should ask your dad to do it. I would do it, too, but, yeah, I think your dad should do it."

"Oh, yes," agrees Sergei. "Jordan is right."

"It's a present for him, though," I tell them and laugh.

"A present like that might make him feel left out," says Jordan.

"Time spent working with you—that's his gift," adds Sergei.

"Okay, I see your point," I say. "But he's been so out of it, I thought he might not want to do it."

"That's exactly why you want him to do it." Jordan stands and walks over to the sink and starts washing a pancake mold for the microwave. "It'll get him out of his head for a minute."

I start mixing a batter. "Okay. Sounds good."

Once I have everything made, Sergei and Jordan head to the farm with coffee containers. I go to wake my dad.

He is so sound asleep when I get there, I don't think I should wake him. It's a tough call. I really don't know how long it's been since he ate. I decide to go back to the galley where I eat a few pancakes and some fruit. (No lettuce, though.)

I wrap up the rest and leave a note for my dad. "Eat something! This plate won't take 'no' for an answer either." It occurs to me that both the plate and I will, in fact, take 'no' for an answer, but I promise I am doing a whole lot more worrying than any plate ever will.

Chapter 68

Today I celebrate the commencement of my 16th set of 365 Earth days. That's what today is. In Florida, I could get a driver's license. Two Earth years from now, I can vote in the U.S. In five, I can have a glass of wine anywhere on Earth. Here, I fly a massive spaceship going about 180 light years per Earth year and I haven't even been in the same room as a glass of wine for my entire life. I'll figure out the driving thing sometime later, I think, as well as the voting and drinking parts.

Sometimes I feel like I have lost everything. Sometimes I feel like my life contains everything and it's getting bigger.

We can see Sol now. Earth's sun. It's visible to the naked eye from the flight deck and getting bigger in appearance every day. It's hard not to keep checking on it. We are almost there.

When you look out toward Earth from the Kepler planets, Earth appears to be almost nothing. The other stars, planets, auroras, and asteroids make a much bigger, better show. They blaze pink, white, orange, and red. The only way the Milky Way would look like spilt milk is if the milk was let loose in space.

But the stars and celestial bodies don't just blaze. They also glow. And spark. And streak. They spread their light. They're fuzzy and round, or squished and oval. They speckle the heavy blanket of darkness.

Space is colorful. You don't get a lot of green. Based on your vids, you Earth folks do not get to know purple like I have gotten to know purple. And red and orange and white and yellow and blue. Every hue of those colors.

As you get closer to the Earth and Earth's sun starts to make itself known—you start to look for Earth itself. But for a long time, you just see Sol, a white light. A yellow, white light. A spot of yellow, white light. Then, finally, the planets become visible.

Most diagrams of Earth's solar system line up the planets like they're on a string. But as we have flown closer to Earth's solar system, we have slowed down and, I can tell you for sure, that the planets look like they are strangers sharing a trip on a spaceship, and must hover and circle around each other—they have no other choice.

Earth's moon looks like a dead piece of Earth, gray and rough. Chalky. Just rocks and dust. But Earth's moon and Earth are tethered together. Not strangers, but partners spinning around.

The Earth is exactly the color of my father's eyes, just as my mother said it would be. That dark blue of oceans. I miss my mother.

Now that we are so close, down becomes a much stronger word to me again. And it means one thing—in the direction of the surface of planet Earth. So I can make the following statement: down there, we will see whirls of white clouds and the brown of mountains. Down there. Down.

I have never done most things people do, except virtually. But I'm about to take a ride from orbit to the Earth.

I'm looking forward to that. And I'm looking forward to sand. Dirt. Rain splattering on my arms. I want to listen to that sound of it plinking on a roof or hull. I want to get to know paint and charcoal and pencil shavings. Do tulips really smell like candy?

I know we're going incredibly fast—but, wow, does this seem slow sometimes.

Chapter 69

We celebrate all the birthdays still, you know, even for those who have left us. It's a way to continue to celebrate and honor the family that we are, the culture we have on the ship.

For this birthday (John-Michael's birthday), we are also marking the official name for Kepler-917 (the beige planet). It's going to be called Goush-MacFarland for Panchi and John-Michael. They would like that, being honored together.

Maybe it should be somber, but at John-Michael's dinner, we are giddy. We are less than a day away from Earth and are slowing to a rate of speed where we can enter an orbit around Earth.

"Safe at home base," says Jordan.

The WSC is planning to send up a shuttle to meet us when we get settled in that orbit. Sergei and I are spending all of our time working on the flight deck. More adjustments have to be made all the time.

We've lowered the ship out of FTL travel now and are making a close pass by Mars—not quite close enough to wave to the scientists stationed there. I made the mistake of suggesting we land on that red planet, but the captain and Dad both shot that down immediately. Dad said, "We don't have the power to go in and out of orbit."

The captain just said, "No."

It's really too late to head for Mars anyway.

We are all busy with the constant work to prepare for Earth orbit, except it doesn't feel like work at all but instead like an intense state of being awake, engaged, and alive. Everything else falls away—grief, worry, anxiety, as well as how quiet the ship is—all of it falls away.

There are more meteors flying by us than usual—way more than we predicted. They are big enough so we can feel it sometimes when they hit, but nothing big enough to worry about right now.

Halfway through the birthday celebration, Sergei straightens up, standing like he's going to recite a poem or give a speech. But he's acting funny, his words are slurred. He says he has a massive headache. Then Dad says something weird: "Are you drunk?" I don't think there's even alcohol on the ship, though I know they could probably make it if they wanted. And hide it from me too, maybe.

Sergei responds, "No, no, I think I need to check my eyes. Everything seems faint. Maybe I'm tired."

Jordan says, "Come back with me to the med unit. I'm worried about you."

"Nyet!" Sergei pushes himself away from us. "Shhhh. I am good. Jus' tired. Tomorrow, I ss- ss- see you again."

"No, Sergei. Let me see you now. Ted, go get an oxygen pack ready in the med unit." Jordan moves around the table and pulls Sergei to him. "I'm getting you back there."

Then Jordan adds, "Dammit. Dammit. Sergei."

Chapter 70

Jordan and my dad are moving Sergei to the medical unit, gently pulling on his arms, legs, clothes. This sort of thing must be harder to do in high gravity. Sergei struggles with them at first, but then he stops pushing Jordan and Dad away. He's kind of limp.

Jordan leans toward me and says this might be a stroke.

A stroke? That could incapacitate Sergei. It could kill him. My body slumps in my seat. I'm shocked. My mouth opens.

Then the ship shudders. And shudders again.

"Rosie!" The captain yells at me. "Get to the flight deck. I think we've been hit with something that damaged the ship." The meteors have been like grains of sand all day, like a sand storm. But this is different.

The captain is way ahead of me, disappearing toward the front of the ship. A quick look around and I'm alone in the galley with the remains of John-Michael's birthday dinner. Napkins, dishes, some blobs of water and crumbs lie on the table; some of this is scattered on the floor.

I pull myself out of the galley, through Sergei's quarters,

past the burnt hallway, and the rest of the way to the front of the ship. I grab and push hard against the sides of portals, bunks, anything to get there faster. When I emerge into the flight deck, the captain is strapping himself into the co-pilot seat.

"Look, Rosie," he starts. "As captain of the ship sometimes I run everything and sometimes I play backup to everyone. This is one of those times I'm going to have to play back-up. You know way more about flying this ship than I do—you've been immersed in the processes with Sergei for months, and your mom and Jack taught you well." He fastens his straps. "Now it's time to be the pilot and chief navigator. Got it?"

That was not a question. I slide into the pilot's seat and strap my body to it. Then I start focusing on the instruments.

A meteoroid smacks into the window on the starboard side, like a diamond out of a cannon. It leaves a mark. Two more hit from that direction, and another on port.

"Captain, we have damage to the windows. Permission to close the starboard flight deck shutter."

"Rosie," the captain says back. "Do what you need to do."

I activate the flight deck starboard and port shutters. They close like the inner membranes of a frog's eye. They're not as clear as the regular windows, but you can still see through them. Frog fog.

"Would you create a voice connection to WSC, please?" I ask the captain. "They should know what's going on. It might change their plans."

And now something hits the back of the ship and throws us off by a couple of millimeters. I won't pause to say this too many times, but being thrown off at all is a big deal.

A voice comes in over the ship's communications console. "This is orbital control, WSC, speaking." The captain pops the button that will keep the two-way link open. We are on speaker with the WSC. Somewhere in the back of my mind

I know that everything I say will be heard and probably recorded. And I also know that I will stop being aware of that fact really quickly. I might say anything. I hope I don't say anything too embarrassing.

Something hits an outer docking ring. I know because there are sensors on it and my screen shows the intensity of the impact. And then there's another impact to a different docking ring. I am not sure, but that might impact our chances to hook up to a WSC shuttle, space station, or anything else flying around out here.

"Hello," I call out because I am not sure what else to say.

"Hello," says a voice with a smile in it. You can hear that. I bet the person talking on the WSC line has kids my age or younger. Maybe not, but I'll take whatever good vibes and affection I can get right now. She does have a nice voice.

"Um." I am so articulate. "Um, um, we are going to want to change the WSC shuttle schedule, the meteor storm is way bigger than predicted."

"What damage have you sustained?" the voice asks.

"We have damage to the flight deck windows and to two of the outer docking rings. I have closed some of the shutters." Then I turn to the captain. "Would you, um, forward any damage errors that show up on the monitor to the WSC orbital control, um, please."

The voice says, "Send them to the general orbital control account and copy me. This is Jen Bosco, I'm the senior person here right now."

I know this person's name. Jen Bosco isn't just the senior person in whatever room she's in down there, she's the senior person at the WSC. She's a little bit like a myth to me. Someone you hear stories about, but never expect to meet. Why is she answering the phone?

"You're answering the phone?" I ask.

"I can answer the phone when I want to," Jen Bosco

answers. "Also, we know when it's the Grimm Explorer on the line. We've been preparing for your return."

"That's good to hear."

Of course, right now, there are way more meteors than anything I've ever seen. And I tell her I have to pay attention to them. The captain and I have to use all of our focus on dealing with the incremental changes to the ship. Some changes are not so incremental.

"Will it be enough to listen to us working?" I ask.

"Yes," Jen Bosco answers. "We will monitor your conversation and, if needed, ask for clarification. We are standing by for your questions and problems as needed."

While the captain pulls together the damage errors and reports them to the WSC, I stay focused on maintaining our planned flight path. We end up shuttering all of the flight deck and launch bay windows.

Then I hear an alarm. The hull is weak in the area of the fire and outside the shuttle launch bay at the back of the ship. There is a red light on the console—it's the "check coordinates" light. I'm just going to have to live with that one for a while because there's nothing I can do about it right now. The red lights on the ship's main environmental system gages are more concerning.

I tell the captain, "Captain, can you look into the main environmental system? If we lose that, you know, nothing else matters. The problem might be electrical. It's hard to tell from here."

The captain unstraps and pulls himself up and out of the chair. My dad shows up at the door. "Ted," the captain calls out. "We need to check the environmental system. And after that look at two places that might have hull damage." Dad and the captain disappear, faces looking at their devices. I'm sure they are syncing up on damage reports and assessments.

I keep working at the helm. The flight deck goes quiet. Really quiet. I'm alone without the captain and my dad.

The alarms stop. The meteor shower continues to subside. I look up and toward Earth through the dulled panes of the lowered flight deck windows. I think it's over.

The captain and Dad reappear in the doorway. When I see them, I first look down at the "check coordinates" light like it's the one constant in the universe. Then I look at the environmental system gages.

Then Jordan joins us. "Sergei has died," he says.

And with that, my friend is gone.

Chapter 71

A new alarm goes off on the console and cuts me off from thinking about Sergei. It's the alarm for the fuel cells. They're low on energy. I haven't even thought about the fuel cells.

Usually, the fuel cells—which are like giant batteries—run off of the nuclear fusion engine which provides all the energy we could ever want or need. Even for FTL travel. Even for 16 years. Even for a relatively-effective ship-wide gravity system. The solar panels contribute to the ship's system too, but that's like blaming one herd of cows for Earth's climate change. Or it's like the amount of fuel an apple contributes to your diet for a week. Sure, it's a part of the picture, but it's a really small part of it.

I yell out of fear and exhaustion. "Dad, the fuel cells are low!"

"Got it, Rosie. It might be a result of the electrical system problems." My dad is right there on top of it.

The captain chimes in, "We need to coordinate. We have a lot happening right now. Rosie, you list the issues you see happening. Then we'll go around the room to see if we have everything in hand." He looks around at the three of us, who, together with him, now constitute "the room."

I pause. "Okay. Here's are the problems I know about. Flight coordinate corrections. Low fuel cells. Possible electrical system damage. Meteor damage. Outer docking ring damage. Environmental system alarm is going off."

"Ted," commands the captain.

"Electrical system is most certainly compromised," says Dad. "To add to that list, I'll say hull damage is possible and needs to be checked."

"Jordan?" asks the captain.

Jordan pauses for a few heartbeats. Then he says, "I don't have any issues to add to that. Except that our crew is under extreme stress and might be suffering the physical effects of that."

The captain takes over. "Rosie, you're where you need to be. Focus on the flight path and piloting the ship. Double-check to see if we should try for the Mars station instead. See if WSC can hook us up with one of the space stations—the docking ring issue might preclude that. Ted, you focus on the electrical system. I'll do a check of the ship's integrity and do a manual pass-through of the ship to clean up any debris. Jordan, use your data to see if we have any imminent physical problems for the crew. Take care of Sergei's body, please." The captain sits down and massages between his eyes. "Then let's meet back here in two hours and we'll do an assessment and assign sleep schedules."

I realize I'm beyond exhausted. I can't wait two hours. "Captain," I say. "May I take a nap right now? I think I'm fading."

"Yes, of course. Set your alarm for two hours. You can get back into it then."

I haul myself to my bunk as the others go toward different areas of the Grimm Explorer to work on their assignments. By the time I have my blanket over my head, I am asleep.

Chapter 72

Two and a half hours later, Dad is rubbing my shoulder over the blanket. "Time to get up, honey. I know it's hard."

It's like pulling myself up from a dark pit, but I make myself conscious. There's my dad's face. There's the curve of the ship above my bunk. The lights are low. I think I never set an alarm.

"Here's some water, Rosie." My dad hands me a container and I immediately start gulping the contents. "As soon as you can, get up to the flight deck. We all need to be working now. We've turned down the gravity by half already, so be careful of that."

I am up on one elbow as I watch him leave our quarters. I don't know if he's slept at all. Then I get up and move to the front of the ship. Everything feels extra bouncy because of the weak gravity. And it seems like they've turned the lights down low all over the ship.

When I get to the front, Dad is already there. I shift into the pilot seat and start assessing our position. My dad's face is turned down looking at his tablet, pulling data and making adjustments. The captain and Jordan come into the flight deck area.

The captain begins. "We have damage to the outside hull in the area of the fire. It's holding for now. But it's a concern because of the damage to the inner hull. The damage to the outer docking rings is extensive and will likely prevent our using them to dock to any shuttle sent up from the WSC or any of the space stations—WSC or commercially owned."

"Captain? I'd like to add something," Jordan says. "Medibot shows we are all living in an atmosphere of reduced oxygen. Could there be oxygen loss?"

My dad adds to Jordan's statements, "What I thought was a possible electrical failure in the environmental system is a definite electrical failure, but it extends beyond the environmental system. I think the reduced oxygen, as important as it is, is part of that larger problem. It's not isolated."

The captain asks, "Do you have a list of repairs we can make?"

"Yes, here it is." My dad taps a couple items on his phone and hands it to the captain.

"Let's split the list between us. Jordan, keep on top of the environmental stats."

When they all leave the flight deck, I look out the window. Shutters retracted, the view is clear. There's the Earth and the Moon, looking more huge than ever and like they are a pair of old friends.

I need to concentrate on the flight corrections. I know my work won't mean anything if we can't breathe. But if we can breathe, we'll need those corrections. I'm going to assume we're going to keep on breathing.

Chapter 73

My dad and the captain have been working on the electrical system for five hours. During that time, Jordan has stationed himself with me, but we each work independently. I only get up to use the latrine, to wash, and to eat. I can feel my legs puff up with inactivity.

Jordan's com goes off and the captain's voice is there, but it's a stressed-out voice—tight, a little higher-pitched than his usual low baritone. "Jordan. Can you pull what's left of the electrical supply inventory and bring it here? We need to patch some things."

"Yes, sir," Jordan responds. He toggles off the com and says to me, "I'm just finishing up here, I'll be with your dad and the captain if you need me."

At this point, I have done, and re-done the calculations for the flight path and communicated them to the WSC. The WSC crew checks and confirms my plan and I am about to start making manual maneuvers.

I engage the thrusters and shift their direction. They swivel into position dictated by the numbers I have put into the program. Then I initiate the first blast of what is supposed to be twenty small blasts to re-orient the ship. When that first blast works, I lean back—relieved. My relief is super short-lived with the second thruster blast, though—that's because it's a non-existent second thruster blast. After the thruster swiveled into position, it did not have any power to fire. I go through my list, making each blast, but making them at a smaller intensity level than planned. Fifteen of the twenty thrusters do not go off. Fifteen. Do. Not. Go. Off.

And I'm going to have to re-do all the calculations.

I'm going to need all the help I can get as fast as I can get it. I activate the com link to the WSC. "Mission control?"

"Mission control, here," comes a male voice.

"This is Rose Marie, on 1GRM-X. Our thrusters are not firing," I respond.

"All the thrusters?" asks the male voice.

"Negative. Fifteen of the thrusters do not appear to be functioning off the main fuel cells. But I have a plan to use the remaining five as much as possible."

"Go ahead and use the five thrusters. Mission control standing by."

I run through the routines to use the remaining thrusters to make the adjustments, but they are not powerful enough and we are still drifting off-course.

The thrusters are powered by electricity off the fuel cells, but I think I can try something else. I think; I hope. I want to run the idea by someone first.

"Mission control?" I call out to the WSC operator.

"Mission control, here. It's Tim Matthews, by the way." The same voice answers.

"Hi, Tim. Thanks for IDing yourself," I respond. "Can I run another idea by you?"

"Sure. Are the remaining thrusters able to compensate for the ones that are not working?" asks Tim.

"No, sir." I tell him. "They aren't strong enough. I thought I might use the solar panels to provide the power. We could try connecting them directly without using the drained fuel cells. Do you have anyone there who is an expert on the panels and how we might re-connect them?"

"We will reach out to a subject matter expert and get them to advise you and the rest of the crew in an hour or two. Mission control out." Tim signs off (temporarily, I hope). I kind of hope Jen Bosco is around next time. I liked working with her.

I take a deep breath. Our oxygen problems are getting worse. The air up here has become kind of close and stuffy, but chilly. Colder than usual. This is not to say that I'm all that cold, but I have never been this cold. My whole life has been pretty much a balmy twenty-two degrees.

I tap the com to see if the captain, Dad, and Jordan have gotten anywhere with the environmental system. "Hello?" I say.

No one answers. Right. I needed to stretch my legs anyway. I unstrap and head to the back of the ship. But first I hit my head on the ceiling. Right. Gravity is turned down.

I find the three of them back near the engine of the ship which is over by the launch bay. They have three banks of electrical wiring pulled out of the hull and into the interior of the ship. They are surrounded by coils of insulated wire of various colors and three different kinds of pliers as well as bits and pieces of circuitry. All three of them are patching wires and redoing the environmental electrical grid. All three look stressed out, faces drawn.

"Dad?" I start.

"Hey, sweetie." He doesn't look up. "I felt the thrusters. Did you get the ship back on track?"

"I moved it some, but we're off course and not all the thrusters are powered anymore. Most of them aren't powered, in fact. I'm trying to shift to the solar panels for power."

"No can do, honey," he responds. Now he looks up at

me, face pale and damp. "We need the solar panels for the environmental system. That's what we're working on now. The fuel cells aren't holding power so well anymore."

"Is there any other power source on the ship?" I ask. "Do we have anything that could make a chemical rocket?"

The captain replies, "No. We do not have an alternate fuel for chemical rockets."

I go back to the flight deck. I might be able to continue using smaller blasts to reorient us. But I also think I need to keep the ship to Earth com connection open with the WSC mission control for this. This is going to take a lot of little bursts. It might not be enough.

I open my phone's com to the rest of the ship before I call WSC. "Hi, all. I'm going to push the ship using what power I can from the fuel cells, so get ready. We have to get this ship back on course. Okay?"

There's a huge silence. "Hello?" I repeat. "Starting another round of thrusters?"

The captain says, "Do a few at a time so we can watch the drag on the fusion engine and fuel cells." His voice gets a little fainter. He must have turned his head. "Jordan, stay on the fuel cell status."

"Let me connect the ship's com to mission control, too, so they know what's going on," I say.

"Mission control? Anyone there? Tim?"

"Hello, this is Tim," comes the response.

"We're losing air somehow, the fuel cells are failing. Not much power for shifting the ship. Solar power is dedicated to the environmental system. We can't use it for the ship's thrusters. Will you stay on the line?"

"Affirmative. We'll keep this connection open for the duration." Good. Tim's going to stay available.

I start making tiny blasts. But each time I use a thruster, the engines drain and do not recover fully. It's a game of diminishing capacity. I hit a burst. The cells do not recover all the way to where they were. I hit a burst. The cells do

not recover all the way. And so on.
    They are getting dangerously low in power.

Chapter 74

"We need to turn off the gravity all the way," blurts out my dad over the ship com.

"Copy that," says Tim.

Great. I'm stuck in the middle of them.

"Let me know when it's off. I'll try a burst after that," I ask.

"You'll know when it's off, Rosie," says my dad.

And I do know when it's off. The floating feeling increases and I rise against the straps on my seat. Now I am directly experiencing part of the reason the straps are there in the first place. "Got it, Dad. Going for a small burst from one of the working thrusters. Ready? Now." I turn on the next burst.

"The power system is not holding," says Jordan. "Oxygen levels have decreased. We need to think of something else."

"I'll stop trying to use the power for moving the ship for now," I say.

Jen Bosco's voice comes out of the connection with the WSC. "What's the status of the outer docking rings? Can we send a local ship out to you? We would need a day to prep."

"Not good, ma'am," the captain says. "The rings are damaged beyond use."

"Sir, ma'am," says Jordan. "We might not have a day left in this ship."

"Dad, Captain—how's our shuttle? Can that take the four of us the rest of the way?" I interject.

"Yes, good idea. Sergei did the maintenance work. We need to double-check it. None of us have worked on it since the two Finch-Hernandez flights," says the captain.

"We're kind of far for the shuttle," says Dad.

"Too far out?" asks the captain.

"I think we're in range, it's something we have to think about," responds my dad.

Jordan is the next voice, "We don't have a lot of time."

"Ted, Jordan—check the remote shuttle diagnostics," orders the captain. "It might be the only way to get out of here."

Jordan repeats, "We don't have—"

"Convert the shuttle bay to air lock, Rosie," interrupts the captain. "Get it as ready as possible while Ted and Jordan run remote checks on it."

I start the process from the flight deck. But I have to get myself all the way down to the other end of the ship, too. So I unstrap and move as fast as I can. When I get there, I check the launch bay controls from there, hoping the status and all the seals are good.

It's usually a five minute process. When ten minutes go by, I start to worry. Is this a result of the power issues? Is there a leak? And there's something else to worry about. There are four bodies stored in there. What does this do to them? Do we have the time to care about bodies—bodies emptied of the people they were?

"Captain—we need to see if there's a leak in the bay. It's going too slowly." I'm yelling to him through two compartments of the ship. The dim light coming from the sick bay and storage goes fully dark.

The captain pushes himself over to me. "We don't have time to check. Can we survive the airlock?"

"We can put on space suits to get out there." I reply. "Jordan can use Sergei's suit. It's probably the closest fit."

"Do it," orders the captain. "Ted, Jordan, get to the shuttle bay. Jordan, get out Sergei's and John-Michael's suits—you might have to see which is better. We're evacuating the ship via the launch bay and shuttle."

Until the captain says the word "evacuating" it hadn't really hit me, yet. Now, I get it. We have to leave. The ship won't support us anymore. Yes, it's a surprising feeling even though Jordan has turned into the voice of doom and keeps reminding us about the limits of the air supply.

The equipment for the space suits is all stored in cabinets outside the lock. I start opening the cabinets and pulling out Jordan's old space suit that was tailored for me. Then I change my mind. Without gravity, they're going to float. I pull out the pieces for the captain and hand them to him. "This is your space suit gear," I tell him.

Dad and Jordan are right there. "Jordan," and I hand him the suits that were made for Sergei and for John-Michael as well as the boots that were made for him. "Sergei's suit is on top, but both sets are there in case you have to switch. And Dad, here."

Finally, I pull out my own suit and boots and say, "I think the shuttle is fine to support us. If we have some issues, we'll still have some air and environment through the suits to keep us going. Jordan, bring the extra suit."

Chapter 75

Each of us starts putting on a space suit. The process takes longer than you think. We have to double-check the way all the parts get assembled. I'm the only one here who has put one on before. A small leak can be deadly.

I pair off with my dad and we go through the procedure. We are halfway dressed in the suits when there is a big boom. Then the ship is quiet.

I mean really quiet. I don't think I knew silence before now. There's always been some vent or fan or air system running.

"That's it," says Jordan.

"Don't stop getting into your suits," urges the captain. "Since we're still breathing, it's not a full breach. We only have a half hour. If there is a full breach, we have 15 seconds."

Dad and I continue the methodical process of putting on pieces of equipment and having each double-checked. The air is really cold now. I see fog every time I breathe out. I am shivering like when I was sick, but I'm not aching.

"Fifteen minutes," calls out Jordan as he and the captain

continue the paired process of getting into their suits.

"How's the suit?" the captain asks Jordan.

"Good. Sergei and I were like brothers in size as well as in, you know, friendship," answers Jordan. "It's tight around the shoulders, but I can live with that."

I'm feeling faint. "I don't feel so good," I tell my dad.

"Hey, just keep going," he responds. "We're almost there."

Once my helmet and gloves are finally on and the suit pressurizes, I feel instantly better. It's warmer too. I look at my dad—he seems fine. Jordan is fumbling with his helmet.

My dad goes to Jordan and helps with his helmet. Then he checks the captain's gear. "You look all set, Andre," he says. "Jordan, let's get these gloves on you."

Jordan leans back like he's feeling faint. "Come on, buddy," says the captain who reaches his gloved hand under Jordan's armpit.

Jordan stays on his feet and we change partners. I find a puncture in the captain's sleeve. "Captain, your suit," I tell him.

"No bother, Rosie," he says. "The skin will make a seal with the fabric."

"But—" I start.

"No time, Rosie," he says. "Open the shuttle bay door." He presses his suit fabric to his arm.

I look at each of them. Yes, we all seem ready. The shuttle bay door opens.

There is a mist in the room. I don't know why. I'm glad I can't smell it. But I can hear a rushing sound. There's definitely a breach somewhere which is why we couldn't get the launch bay converted to a pressurized state.

We push, float, and pull ourselves to the shuttle door and Dad hits the button to open it. "Get in first, Rosie."

I climb into the co-pilot seat.

"No," says the captain. "You know where you need to be."

I get out of that seat and into the pilot seat, then start putting on the straps. As soon as all four of us are on the shuttle, I close the door. It's like an eye that blinks and never opens again.

I initiate the startup sequence. Once it powers up, I tap on the shuttle's com and connect to WSC. "1GRM-X Shuttle one, here," I say. "We have boarded Little Bear and are ready to start the take-off process."

"Mission control." The voice is Jen Bosco's again.

I continue the preparation to leave. I command the ship to open the bay's outside door remotely. The doors grind open.

The captain is checking his arm.

Jordan asks about it. "What happened to your arm?"

"The small piece of exposed skin feels burned," says the captain. "I think that's it. The suit sealed itself to my arm."

"Okay. That was lucky," says Jordan. "I don't think any of us knew what was going to happen with that."

The WSC technicians mutter and chat and talk to us over the com constantly.

As we are about to leave, I hear a familiar voice.

"We advise leaving the ship before the doors are fully open," says Jen Bosco. "Do not wait. There is a concern with the nuclear fusion engine."

"Like what kind of concern? An explosion?" I say.

"That is extremely unlikely," says Jen Bosco.

"But possible," says my dad.

"Yes, but possible," affirms Jen.

And then no one is talking, on the shuttle or at mission control. This silence is broken by a well-known voice. "Hi, Rosie." It's Ethan Junior.

I didn't know that Ethan Junior had been invited into the control room. Ethan Junior has a deep voice that I haven't heard in a long time. It is even deeper than it was, I think. It's been awhile since we had a live voice call. Maybe it was when the vid went viral?

"Ethan Junior!" I call out to him.

"Yeah," he says. "I'm here."

I can't help but smile. Having him there is a good thing. Everything seems better now. Even with the possible nuclear fusion engine explosion.

Little Bear is on a kind of large arm that extends to move it out of the ship. That extension arm grinds, too. It's not supposed to do that.

We are halfway out the door—front end in space, back end in the launch bay—and the extension arm stops. I will have to get the shuttle out of the launch bay manually.

I fire up the engines while the shuttle is still attached and hanging like a tongue from the ship. Maybe that's not a good plan, but I don't want to hit the floor of the launch bay. Then I disengage from the extension arm. There is a long creak and screech as the coupling ring scratches the bottom of the shuttle. Okay, it's not the floor of the launch bay, but that is not great either.

I push the shuttle's thrusters giving them a quick, gentle burst and we move a little bit further out of the ship. I cut the thrusters and let us drift out a little, not wanting to be on full power while any part of Little Bear is still in the ship.

Another small burst. Another. And we are far enough out to go to full power. I bring our speed up. And we are fully free of the ship. I'm not sure where the ship will drift. I don't know what's still functioning. The ship is cut off from me, no longer a home base. I can't even look back to see it. I don't have the resources to look back. There's no mirror for that, no window in the back of the shuttle. So there it is. Story of my life. No chance to say goodbye.

This means we're leaving the bodies of my mom and my friends behind. Their days were my days. My days were theirs. That is, except when Sergei spent a year on Moscow-time. Then, his nights were my days. I could more easily leave a part of my brain behind right now. But I have no choice. Story of my life.

Chapter 76

It's not like Little Bear was pre-programmed for this. There's no autopilot. It had programming for some functions for landing on the Kepler planets—nothing for landing on Earth.

The first thing is to point ourselves toward Earth because, no, we are not currently on track with intercepting it. You'd think it would be hard to miss. But we are next to the moon instead and hanging there pointing toward it, Earth's biggest, oldest satellite.

Speaking of satellites, when I look around at Earth, I can see about fifteen of them. It looks like all kinds of stuff up here. I don't even know what all of it is. I guess I'm used to planets where there's nothing going on in orbit except the Grimm Explorer.

I have to figure out a few things right away. First, how much power and fuel do we have? Second, how much air do we have? Third, how much can I maneuver? And of course, four, what am I forgetting? Environment? Programming? Com with WSC mission control?

"Captain, we have operational fuel cells," I report. "I'm

going to test the shuttle engine to make sure the fuel cells can stay powered."

"Excellent," replies the captain. "Jordan and I will work on assessing the environmental system. We had that issue at Finch-Hernandez. The shuttle performed well after the accident, but I want to test everything. Ted, assist Rosie."

My dad is already in the co-pilot seat. And that is a good thing for me, just, you know, psychologically. As I start to check the engine and fuel cells, Dad asks, "What do you want me to do?"

"Get mission control connected up to the com, again, please," I answer.

"Mission control?" He's got it up right away.

"Mission control, here." I think that's Tim's voice.

"We are safely in the shuttle," says my dad, "and we have moved away from 1GRM-X but we have to re-align. Yes, Rosie? What's the plan for navigation?"

"I'm testing that right now," I add. "The shuttle is facing the moon and has to turn around to head toward Earth."

Dad says, "Can we swing Little Bear around the moon, you know, like in the vids? Use that centripetal force? Or wait, is that centrifugal?"

Tim's voice comes through the com. "Centrifugal. But it's moot. You don't have positioning or the initial momentum to do that. What's Little Bear?"

"Look," I interject. "We are first going to have to get further away from the ship and get pointed in the right direction, you know, toward Earth."

"Little Bear is our name for the shuttle," says Dad. "Like we call the ship the Grimm Explorer. Melissa had names, stories for all the robots and the shuttle. She used them in stories for Rosie when we were at Kepler-917."

Wait. What? That's where Itchy and Scratchy and Little Bear come from? Bookmark that thought. "I don't remember that," I tell my dad, looking at him.

"You were pretty small, Rosie," he answers. "There was

a pop song that went along with it."

"Can we just drift and use gravity to pull us home?" asks Jordan, the voice of reality.

I glance back at Jordan who, with the captain, is sitting behind us. We are two by two. "That would take a long time and we're being pulled by other things, too," I answer. "We'd have to think about how long we can survive in the shuttle without water and food, that sort of thing. You know, and the air might run out. We're occupied at full capacity, but it's not meant to be a long-term vehicle. Right now we're in the outer layers of Earth's atmosphere. Or are you thinking we should fly ourselves close enough and then we can just fall onto Earth's surface?" I am thinking out loud here.

"Okay, that could be a plan," I continue to talk through my thoughts to no one in particular. I hope they will correct me if I say something that doesn't make sense. "We have to avoid things mostly. Avoid our own ship first. Avoid all the satellites and space junk up here." Wow, that statement begs repeating. There is a lot of junk up here.

I continue, "If we get past all that, um, where do we want to land? I think we won't have to crash land. Not sure if we want to come down on water. Mission control? Recommended locations for a landing? Someplace uninhabited? What would a splashdown landing look like?"

"Hey, can we land on the moon and wait for pick-up?" asks my dad.

I guess we are now in a free-for-all idea session. "Same problem with drifting toward Earth. Little Bear isn't meant for regular habitation and they wouldn't be able to get up here for a few days," I reply. Since it's a brainstorming session I can just shoot down other people's ideas, yes?

Tim agrees with me. "Right," he says. "You guys should come to us. A splashdown landing on Earth means more risks once you've landed. Hitting on the ground, on the other hand, you're equipped for. Um, I mean landing on the ground. Not hitting. But that is still likely the optimal strategy. We have a space center out in Arizona. Maybe head for the Phoenix, Arizona airport." He throws out a question for those nearby him in the mission control room on Earth. "Thoughts?"

Ethan Junior comes on—I'm glad he's still there. "Anything in Florida? Something on the coast? Orlando airport?"

"Wait. Disney World is on the coast of Florida now?" interrupts my dad.

"Eh, near enough," says Tim.

"So the Cape is out?" I say.

"Honey," an unknown woman's voice says, "we lost Cape Canaveral a long time ago."

I'm really weak on what cities are where on Earth. I guess I wasn't paying attention when the planet was light years away.

The woman continues. "Orlando airport is a good idea, though. So we have a couple places in the United States that are good options. Both Phoenix and Orlando have a space center and an airport."

"I understand. So once I get the shuttle turned around, I'll aim for the United States." I reply.

"Yeah, honey," she answers me, "but getting out of space is the most important thing. Once that's done, we'll figure the rest of it out, don't worry. We'll be fine if you head for any city—there's going to be at least one airport there."

Don't worry? I'm not sure if she thinks she's talking to a little kid or what.

I fire the jets on the starboard of the shuttle, but not so much that I'll flip us. I'm trying to get away from the Grimm Explorer and face Earth. This is a long process and I'm working off of what I can see more than anything— that's flying by visual information and not so much by coordinates.

The Grimm Explorer is drifting. So I fire a long burst to get away from it, but we're still heading for the moon and, no, I don't have enough energy to get us in the right position to go around the moon like a slingshot (with us as the rock) all the way back to Earth.

"I'm going to fly between the moon and the ship for a while," I announce.

"What's your thinking?" asks the captain.

"I'm having trouble getting out of the shadow of the Grimm Explorer," I answer. "And I need to do that before I make any other plans for Little Bear."

Jordan, who must have been keeping one eye on the environmental system, speaks up, "Temperature is dropping slowly."

"What?" says the captain. "Ted, what are the fuel cells doing?"

"I think they're at diminished capacity, like the cells on the ship." My dad shifts around to look at them. "We might be at the end of life cycle. They are functioning though. Things are not as bad as they were on the ship."

That makes my job much more urgent. "Mission control," I say. "I'm going to make two basic maneuvers. One, to continue getting away from the ship. Then I'm going to head straight for Earth. I might not be able to pick and choose our landing at all."

"Let's minimize power usage," suggests my dad.

"Good idea," says the captain. "What can we do that will have an effect? Most of the systems are important either for flight or for keeping us alive."

"I think everything will help us," I say.

"How about reducing the heat," offers Jordan.

"Yes, do that," orders the captain. "Turn down the thermostat to twelve. We can adjust from there as needed. You will feel cool, but it shouldn't be terrible."

Dad taps the number into the environmental control.

The fuel cells are actually doing kind of okay. They seem to be able to hold about seventy-five percent of their original capacity. That should be plenty. We don't have to get back to the ship or anything. But I'm still going to take whatever help I can get in the form of reduced energy usage.

To say that we are all still tense is an understatement. But at the moment, I am pushing Little Bear hard toward a point out in space that is neither the moon nor the Earth. That feels so wrong. I would compare it to heading west to go around a mountain when you want to go south. (But what do I know about the feeling of heading west or wanting to go south. I'm guessing here. It's probably like that.)

Fifteen minutes of sustained acceleration gets us pretty much where we want to be. We're free of immediate danger of hitting the ship. We are also "free" of a great deal of the Earth's gravity and continue to be "free" of heading to the Earth.

"Now, we turn," I tell everyone. "I'm not planning to aim for anything in particular. Maybe just a landmass."

We're over the dark part of the planet. The nighttime part. It is easy to see a few things as I turn Little Bear around. First, we're everywhere. And by "we," I mean people. There are lights on every land mass. The parts without cities are small enough to be islands. You could say that they—the empty parts with no cities—seem to be there only because someone at some point must have put up a fence and said: here are no people, the same way a park in a city might be there only because it was drawn on a map that way. Wilderness could not exist here except as a kind of zoo. Caged wilderness.

Next, I can tell where all the coasts are, where roads are. White and yellow lights define the edges of the oceans. Straight lines of these lights are most likely the highways and they lead into blotches of light. It's all very well defined. Are we so afraid of the dark? What's wrong with darkness? I don't think I could get lost on the Earth if I wanted to, if I had a map, that is.

Jordan is in back fiddling with his phone. I hear the captain ask, "What are you doing?"

Jordan says, "I'm seeing if it will connect to a satellite or something terrestrial."

My dad is laughing at him. "Not in airplane mode, huh? I think we're too far out."

Whatever they're talking about, I have to guide us somewhere. But even in the darkness I can make out the northern part of Africa and the Mediterranean Sea. (Thank you, highway lights.) Italy's stubby leg and Greece and Turkey are appendages hanging in there. According to the map overlay, the big body of water is where the Mediterranean joins the Black Sea and the Caspian Sea with a few islands and peninsulas.

We're high up, but I'm angling Little Bear down into the atmosphere. We've gotten past reentry and are hurtling through what one might have to go ahead and call "air."

It looks like we're going to come in way past Africa or the Mediterranean. We are too far north to be in the Middle East. Too far east to be over Europe. I want to be well away from any water.

I think I need to be more selective now. "Dad, can you see if mission control has any airport ideas over here? We are way north of the Mediterranean and the Black Sea."

"Mission control, got a question for you," says Dad into the com system. "We're about to enter Russian airspace."

"You need permission?" comes the woman's voice.

"We first need to know what airports we can go to. Should we get permission?" asks Dad.

"Well, sweetie." She calls me honey and she calls my dad sweetie. "It'd be polite. And might prevent y'all from getting shot out of the air."

"Not sure if we have time for polite," answers my dad. "You guys might. Here's a plan. Please give us a list of airports and alert everyone at those airports who needs to know that we might be coming in for a visit."

"Dad." I want to make a request. "We should go to Moscow. We're really close."

"Can you do it?" says the captain.

"I can," I answer.

Sweetie Hon (that's what I call her now) comes on the com and says, "I hear y'all and I've got some airports here. But I'll start with Sheremetyevo International Airport. That's a Moscow airport. Latitude and longitude are 55°58'22"N 037°24'53"E."

I swear her accent sounds fake and it is bugging me. Enough that this accent and why anyone would fake an accent is what I'm thinking about. I need to focus.

"Okay, got it," I say to her. "Can you do something else for me? Two things really. Can you contact Lilya Dmitrievna Petrova? That's Sergei's mom. She lives around Moscow somewhere. Would you see if she's available? It might be nice for her to see us when we land. I'm not sure what she can do, but I'd like to let her know we're coming."

"Honey," says the lady, "that's a mighty fine idea. We'll get someone on that. You said there were two things you needed?"

"Yeah," I answer. "I'm not sure who's in charge of this, but I want to make a kind of final request before we try to land a space shuttle at a commercial airport without any landing gear. Let this be my last bequest in case we don't make it."

"Yes, honey," she says. I am more worried that she isn't trying to fight me on my pessimism. How dangerous does she think this is?

"Okay, I want you guys to name Kepler-804 after Sergei. It should be called Petrov. That was the one of the planets he walked on and I think it would be the right thing to do. I'm not sure how it happens, though. I just wanted to make the request before it's too late." I take a deep breath. Okay, now there will be absolutely no more thinking about how it might be "too late" anymore.

My arms and body have been getting heavier this whole time. It's getting tiresome to lift them. I think that we're near full gravity. So, this is going to be a main feature of my new life. A new friend I'm going to call "one full g."

With that thought, I realize I'm going to have to figure out the landing process. I'm not sure how well they're going to like having space thrusters on their runway. We'll see.

Chapter 77

There are three airports around Moscow. One in the north. One on the east side. One on the west side. I've trained Little Bear on the airport at the north, the first one that Sweetie Hon lady mentioned to me.

I've decided not to use the thrusters for landing. I'm going to slide in on the belly of the shuttle and the airport is going to be on hand with their equipment for stopping airplanes and for stopping fires. I hope airports have that sort of thing.

"Here's the plan," I start to say. "We're going to bring Little Bear down as low and slow as I can. The northern airport is my target. I hope the Sheremetyevo airport is ready for us."

The captain speaks, "Mission control, what are the protocols for this? Can we release the thrusters early? Is there anything we can use for drag?"

"Negative—since they aren't chemical. But we might be able to use them for drag or skids." I answer him without waiting for Sweetie Hon.

"Like on a sled?" asks the captain.

"I think," I say. "Yeah. Like that." Why is he asking the one person in the shuttle who has never been on a sled? Oh, yeah, I'm the pilot.

We are circling the airport now. I'm trying to reduce speed and figure out the best approach. But we're also trying to give Sheremetyevo International Airport a chance to get ready. Clear the runway. Get fire crews in. Get the fire trucks ready. Apparently they do, in fact, have firefighters and fire equipment ready. I really hope there are no fires.

My problems continue to feature the level of gravity around here and I'm sweating hard now, skin all covered in water. The air seems moist. I'm hoping that's what it's supposed to be. It's cold. It's cold and I'm sweating.

Then, our environmental alarms start to go off. Maybe one of the fans isn't working. Is that okay? A broken fan can be a disaster in space. I'm not sure here. I'm not even sure what's going wrong. A temperature plunge killed my mom and Jackie. That might not be a problem at all here. How extreme could an ordinary Earth temperature be? Isn't it summer here? So in addition to the concentration and sweat and cold, there is a heartbeat blaring going off. *Nnnnn. Nnnnn. Nnnnn. Nnnnn.*

And it's not helping with the tension at all.

Finally, it is time. There is no point to circling the city anymore. The dawn is breaking over the buildings—very many of them, standing tall-shouldered or squat like piles of concrete. All the land around here is sectioned into squares. Everything is big.

I focus on the landing strip and bring Little Bear down gently, thrusters swiveled to parallel the ground. They skim the asphalt first, I hold it there, sparks flying, and then drop the rest of the shuttle to the ground.

We skid. We slide. Little Bear spins around a little, back end wagging one way then another.

Then Little Bear is on the ground. We are no longer in motion. The door opens up—that long sleeping eye. Air rushes in. A crowd is running up to us. I sit back feeling like a limp cloth.

I have only one thought: This place smells weird.

Chapter 78

Should I look forward to being in a home that is more than three bunks stacked up between two bulkheads? I don't know. The three bunks are what I know as home— and it's a place that has the same emotional weight as anyone else's home, I think.

And the flight deck has been my school. And my crewmates are my family. Everything in my universe was right there in the ship. Most of that is gone.

In its place, right here, there are lots of shouting voices. I hear a woman call out, yelling in Russian (like everyone else). But she says something like, "Matz Sergeya." I know that voice. I've heard it fuss and care about someone before.

There is the face of the old woman who belongs to that voice. She has Sergei's chin, and somehow, his eyes. And she is smiling hard at me with everything she's got. And she is crying, too.

I am smelling all the smells in this new place. There are smells I know like grease, oil, ammonia, smoke, copper, and plastic. And there are a lot of smells here that are moist, hair-like and skin-like and I don't know what else. They are like new colors. New shades on the spectrum.

I'm being lifted to a stretcher that rolls forward when I land on it. One full g presses down like a heavy blanket. My heart pushes my sloshing blood around my body. I have to close my eyes again. Then I inhale it all and exhale.

I better be ready to begin something new. Something really, really new.

ACKNOWLEDGMENTS:

Thank you to the team at Brick Cave Media and for the special patience shown by publisher Bob Nelson when he committed to this novel and saw the project through. Additional special thanks goes to Sharon Skinner, Harmony Nelson, and Anne Lind for their careful work. And thank you to the amazing artist Bryan Christopher Moss for created the astonishing cover art. He exceeded what I thought was possible.

My appreciation for the aforementioned wonderful people is boundless. But I must mention this book was written for my two children, Andrew and Carolyn. They are the primary force of good in my life and everything is better because they are in it with me.

Also, I'd like to thank my mother, Joan Robertson, who never read science fiction until I wrote this book and emailed an early draft of it to her. She taught her children to read, took us on innumerable trips to the library, always indulged our eclectic tastes in reading material, and is a genius at the arts of language, love, and card games. Thank you, Mom.

Furthermore, I'd like to include every writer I know. Author Scott Woods leads this list of important contributors to my life as a writer because of our complicated and joyous friendship, our plots and schemes (realized and yet-to-be-realized), and of course our lunchtimes. Here's to more of all of that!

Author Photo Credit: Olivia K. James

ABOUT THE AUTHOR:

Louise Robertson graduated from Oberlin College and earned an MFA in Creative Writing from George Mason University. She is an award winning poet and makes her living as a web developer. Originally from the Washington, D.C. area, she now lives in Central Ohio with her two kids, a cat and a pit-bull. This is Robertson's first novel.